When h... ...ath feathere... ...eck. It instantly created a warm shiver up and down her spine and took considerable effort to stifle.

It had been a long while between men, she thought. Though she told herself that all she was after was earthshaking, teeth-jarring sex, down deep she knew she still had to feel something—respect, admiration, a more than passing attraction, *something*—for the men she went to bed with.

For one reason or another, it had been a long time since she'd "felt" anything at all.

That certainly wasn't the case now.

Dear Reader,

My parents never tried to set me up with anyone. My mother liked having me around, so she was in no hurry for me to marry. My father's plans entailed having me help raise my brothers, and once they were married, I was to enter a nunnery. I'm serious. I had to find my Prince Charming all by myself (which I did).

Today there is never enough time, so a little help finding Mr. Right should be welcome. But having a mother's seal of approval stamped on a man can make a daughter run in the opposite direction—unless she *has* to deal with him. This is Jewel Parnell's situation. As a private investigator she needs to go where the job is, and Christopher Culhane has one for her: find his late sister's ex-husband, because there's the small matter of a half-orphaned boy who needs caring for. Jewel takes the job because she needs it. She ultimately stays because she needs *him*—even if Christopher has her mother's blessing.

I hope you like this little story. I thank you for reading and, as ever, I wish you someone to love who loves you back.

Marie Ferrarella

FINDING HAPPILY-EVER-AFTER

MARIE FERRARELLA

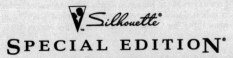

SPECIAL EDITION

Published by Silhouette Books

America's Publisher of Contemporary Romance

SILHOUETTE BOOKS

ISBN-13: 978-0-373-65542-7

Recycling programs
for this product may
not exist in your area.

FINDING HAPPILY-EVER-AFTER

Visit Silhouette Books at www.eHarlequin.com

Printed in U.S.A.

Books by Marie Ferrarella

MARIE FERRARELLA

This *USA TODAY* bestselling and RITA® Award-winning author has written almost two hundred books for Silhouette and Harlequin Books, some under the name of Marie Nicole. Her romances are beloved by fans worldwide. Visit her Web site at www.marieferrarella.com.

To
Jacinta
who won Nik's heart.
Welcome to the family.

Chapter One

He was accustomed to some disorder. It was there, on his desk, in his office at the university. But that was a controlled disorder. If pressed, Christopher Culhane knew exactly how to lay his hands on almost any textbook in his extensive library, be it math or one of the physics disciplines, as well as on any notes that he'd jotted down in the past six to nine months.

This, however, he thought as he looked around what he assumed was the living room, had to be what the inside of Dorothy's house had looked like immediately after the twister had landed it on top of the Wicked Witch of the East.

Maybe even worse, he silently amended. He'd always known that Rita, his younger sister, wasn't much for housekeeping. Growing up, she'd never been able to keep her room in any semblance of order despite their mother's numerous pleas and threats to come in with a bulldozer. Looking back, Rita's room had been downright neat in comparison to what he was seeing now.

How could a sane person live like this? The answer to that troubled him on several levels.

With a suppressed sigh, Chris scrubbed his hands over his face, trying very hard to pull himself together. The past thirty-six hours had been one hell of an emotionally draining ride. A ride that he fervently hoped to God he'd never come close to having to go through again.

"Are you okay, Uncle Chris?" a small, inordinately adult-sounding voice asked, fear vibrating in every syllable.

His nephew, Joel, peered at his face with blatant concern. Joel was small and slight for his age, which made him look even younger than five years old. But the moment he opened his mouth, he negated that impression and sounded like an old man trapped in a child's body.

"You're not having a headache or anything, are you?" he wanted to know. His brown eyes were wide with worry.

Chris shook his head sadly. "No."

Given what the boy had been through, Chris thought, it was a legitimate question, as was the obvious anxiety that surrounded it. According to the story Joel had related, both to the police and then to him, his mother had complained about an excruciating headache just before she collapsed on the floor.

Unlike all the other times she'd fallen down because alcohol or drugs—or both—had temporarily gotten the better of her, this time Rita Johnson did not open her eyes no matter how hard Joel shook her, pleading with her to wake up.

But the brain aneurysm that had ruptured with no apparent warning, other than an overwhelming headache minutes before snuffing out Rita's life, had other ideas.

It was Joel who called 911 and Joel who had told the policeman summoned to the hospital about his mother having a brother in the area. The boy had solemnly added that his mother "didn't want Uncle Chris coming around 'cause he didn't like what she was doing."

Chris had gotten the news just as he finished teaching his last physics class of the day. The dean's administrative assistant had handed him a note asking him to call Blair Memorial Hospital and speak to a Dr. MacKenzie. The sparse message only said that it was about his sister.

An icy feeling had passed over him as he'd dialed the number on the paper.

It had gone downhill from there.

Almost three years had gone by since he'd last seen Rita. That had been her choice. Despite slurring her words, Rita had made that perfectly clear. She'd angrily shouted for him to get out of her house and out of her life, that she'd had "enough to deal with without having you always staring down your disapproving nose at me!"

Trying to reason with her had been useless. He'd had to satisfy himself with covertly driving by the house every so often to catch a glimpse of his nephew and assure himself that the boy was doing all right.

The checks he sent regularly for the boy's care partially saw to that. He knew that his sister did love her child. She wouldn't have allowed him to starve or do completely without. He also knew that if he tried to police her, she'd do something to spite him, so the best method in this case was to give her money earmarked for Joel and stand back. He could only hope that, in her own strange way, Rita gave the boy the emotional support he needed.

Arriving at the hospital to identify his sister, Chris struggled with his own emotions. He had just turned away from Rita's lifeless body when he saw the huge, sad brown eyes looking at him from beneath the thick fringe of dark brown hair. The last time he'd been in the same room with Joel, the boy had been a little more than two years old and already on his way to being a prodigy.

Mourning the fact that this was all such a huge waste of a life, Chris approached the boy slowly. Even though he had conducted himself with exceptional maturity up to this point, Joel was still a five-year-old who had just lost his mother and needed comforting.

Chris had no idea how to talk to someone that young.

He dealt exclusively with adults, and had for some time now. Children were just short human beings he occasionally noted as being part of the background or scenery, like flowers or benches or buildings. He had no direct contact with any of them. He was completely unprepared to break the news to the boy that his mother had died ten minutes after she'd been brought to Blair Memorial.

As it turned out, he didn't have to say very much at all. Joel had looked up at him with stoic, old eyes and said rather than asked, "My mother's dead, isn't she?"

When he'd answered his nephew haltingly in the affirmative, Joel slowly nodded his head. He was amazingly self-contained. In the day and a half that they'd been together since then, he still hadn't heard the boy cry. He was beginning to think that he never would.

It was eerily unnatural.

At a loss as to his next move, Chris had brought Joel back to the home that the boy had shared with his mother. He was utterly astonished at the chaotic scene that met him the moment he unlocked the door. Though it might have once been confined to a small area, the unbridled mess now spread out until it invaded every room in the house. There were newspapers stacked high in the corners, decaying food left on paper plates that turned up in the most unlikely places. And layers of dirty laundry seemed to be scattered everywhere.

The moment they walked in, Joel instantly began to pick things up. The systematic way he moved about told Chris that Joel was the one who tried, albeit unsuccessfully, to put things in order, not Rita. The boy obviously needed the semblance of some kind of order, especially now, when it was his very life that was in chaos. So, the first thing Chris did, right after calling the closest funeral parlor to make arrangements, was to place a call to a local cleaning service.

To his surprise, the woman who answered said they could be there the next morning. Sooner, she assured him kindly, if need be. There was no extra charge for speed. Because he was emotionally wiped out, Chris opted for the morning.

"I'm sorry about the mess," he apologized to the woman who appeared on the doorstep bright and early, armed with a warm smile and a willing crew. The woman, a Ms. Cecilia Parnell, came in first and quietly surveyed what she must have viewed as the aftermath of a blitz attack.

Cecilia smiled in response to the tall, good-looking young man's words, doing her best to melt away any outer discomfort on her client's part.

"Don't be. If there wasn't a mess, you wouldn't be needing my company's services and we'd all be selling tools in a hardware store," she told him cheerfully. She made her way around the stacks of papers, touching things at random as if to get a feel for what needed to be done and how long it would take. "If you don't mind my asking, how long has it been since you—?" She allowed her voice to trail off, not actually saying the word *cleaned* in case he would find it offensive and think that she was in any way criticizing him.

"Oh, it's not my house," Chris informed her quickly. The glut of clutter embarrassed him. "The house is my sister's."

His sister, Cecilia thought, would never give Martha Stewart a run for her money. "And you want to surprise her?" she guessed.

Chris felt his heart twist inside his chest. He shouldn't have stood on ceremony. He should have come over, should have insisted that he be part of Rita's life. Who knows? She might still be alive if he had, he thought as guilt tore off huge, jagged pieces of him.

"It's too late for that," he said. The moment the words were out, Chris realized how enigmatic that had to have sounded to the woman. She was looking at him curiously. He took a breath and explained, "My sister just died."

Sympathy instantly swept over Cecilia, her mother's heart going out to the young man. "Oh, I'm so sorry." She looked around again. Behind her, she heard Kathy and Ally, two of her carefully selected crew, setting up their equipment. Horst was bringing in the industrial-strength vacuum cleaner and muttering something to himself in German. "So you're trying to clean the house up in order to sell it?" She needed to know what his intentions were in order to ascertain just how deeply they were to clean. It was a hard real-estate market these days. A house up for sale had to sparkle right down to the support beams. Even her best friend, Maizie, who could sell hamburgers to a vegetarian, complained about it.

"No!" Quiet up until now, Joel jumped up the moment he heard the word *sell.* He looked stricken as he tugged on Chris's arm. "Don't sell it! You *can't* sell it. This is my home."

There was no way he intended to cause the boy any further pain. Awkwardly, Chris put his arm around the extremely thin shoulders. "I'm not selling the house, Joel. I just want you to be able to walk around here without bumping into things. Or coming down with anything," he added under his breath. He was fairly certain there were three kinds of mold growing in the kitchen alone. Possibly four.

Cecilia quickly connected the dots. "Your nephew?" she asked her client kindly.

He nodded. His arm still around Joel's shoulders, he moved him slightly forward. "This is Joel," he told the woman charged with what amounted to turning straw into gold.

Surprised when the boy offered his hand, Cecilia solemnly shook it. "Pleased to meet you, Joel." She raised her eyes to Chris's face. "And the boy's father?"

Ah, the million-dollar question. "Haven't a clue," he answered, swallowing a sigh. The moment he'd assessed the situation, he'd put in for a two-week leave of absence, citing a family emergency. He hoped it was enough. "Finding him is going to be my first order of business— right after getting this place habitable again."

Oh, yes, dear God, yes! Cecilia had stopped listening after her client had uttered the words *finding him.* Finally, Cecilia thought as relief wove its way through her.

Just when she thought it would never happen for her, or rather, for her daughter, Jewel, it appeared as if lightning were *finally* going to strike. Both of her best friends had miraculously managed to find men for their independent, career-minded daughters among the clientele their businesses serviced.

It was Maizie's plan initially, and Maizie's future son-in-law came to her looking for a house and a pediatrician for his daughter. She sold him the first and introduced him to the second—who just happened to be her daughter, Nikki. Theresa found Jackson when she catered a dinner for him. Theresa's daughter, Kate, and Jackson were going to be married soon, as well.

As for her, she'd given up all hope of finding someone for Jewel. But now she had her chance. Christopher Culhane not only needed his house cleaned, he needed help finding someone—which was Jewel's forte.

Incredibly excited, Cecilia smiled. Karma had finally found her.

"I know a very good private investigator if you're interested." She did her best to sound nonchalant, even though her heart had just gone into overdrive, taking her pulse with it.

The relieved expression on her client's face had her almost giddy. Cecilia had a *very* good feeling about this.

Jewel smelled a rat.

Much as she would have liked to say, "Thanks but no thanks," when the offer had been presented to her, she wasn't exactly in a position to turn down business when it came her way. Even if the referral *had* come from her mother.

She sighed as she drove to the address she'd hastily written down after her conversation with her mother. There was no denying that times were tough for PIs these days. Suspicious wives were deciding that, for the time being, it was better to live with unfounded fears than to pay to find out that those qualms were right on the money because that would only lead to a divorce. And divorce, for now, was just too expensive.

Since most of Jewel's money came from shadowing

cheating spouses, that didn't leave very much for her to do. Before her mother had called her with this case, she had actually been debating asking her if the cleaning service her mom ran needed any part-time help. She hated being idle, not to mention running the risk of falling behind in her monthly bills.

This job was like a stay of execution—with a bonus. For once she didn't have to trail anyone to a sleazy motel and wind up feeling as if she needed to take a shower because of what she'd had to witness and record.

Still, the referral *had* come from her mother and she knew all about the pact that her mother had made with her lifelong best friends. All three of them—Maizie, Theresa and her mother—were determined to get their daughters married. Her mother, and consequently, *she*, was the last woman standing.

That did *not* bode well for someone who valued her privacy and her life as much as Jewel did.

"This is legitimate?" she'd asked her mother not only over the phone, but in person, as well. Having swung by her mother's office to see her face-to-face, she'd scrutinized the older woman for any telltale signs of this being a setup.

Cecilia Parnell had sworn to the name and address' authenticity, ending with the ever popular, "If you can't believe your mother, who can you believe?"

What made this so-called case somewhat suspect was that her mother had given her an address, rather than a phone number.

What was *that* about?

Jewel would have preferred calling first, but her

mother had said that the man was in dire need of a private investigator, so calling him, rather than coming directly over, was just an extra, unnecessary step.

What made it more suspect was that her mother had taken it upon herself to arrange the initial meeting, saying, "It's not as if you've got all that much taking up your time these days, right? There's no schedule for you to reshuffle."

Sad, but true, Jewel thought.

She would have loved to demur and contradict her mother's assumption, except that she really did hate lying unless it was in the line of duty to secure information for a client.

Besides, her mother had an uncanny ability to know when she was lying. There was no point in even trying.

So here she was, pulling into the client's driveway on a fall morning, about to take a case partly against her better judgment. But what choice did she have? None, that's what, she thought darkly.

Getting out of her well-maintained vehicle, she walked up to the front door and rang the bell.

Maybe it wouldn't be so bad, she reasoned, mentally crossing her fingers.

When the door opened, Jewel found herself meeting the gaze of the most solemn-looking child she'd ever seen.

The boy appeared to be waiting for her to speak first.

"Hi," she said brightly.

There wasn't even a hint of a smile on the small, sad-looking face. But, apparently a well-mannered child, the boy did echo her greeting back at her, albeit devoid of any cheer.

"Hi."

Obviously, the bulk of the conversation, at least for now, was going to rest with her, Jewel thought. She smiled at him and resisted the urge to stroke his silky-looking hair. Instead, she squatted down to his level so that they could be eye-to-eye.

"I'm Jewel. What's your name?"

The little boy shook his head, his dark hair swinging almost independently. "I can't tell you."

That took her aback for a second. And then she understood. "Because you can't talk to strangers," she realized. "Good for you," she praised. The boy continued looking at her with the oldest eyes she'd seen in quite a while. "I'm here to see, um—" Jewel looked down at the paper she was holding. She'd made her mother spell the last name so she'd get it right. "A Christopher Culhane." She folded the paper into a small ball with her thumb as she looked back at the boy. "That's your dad I'm guessing."

The boy shook his head from side to side.

"I'm his uncle," a man supplied for him, coming to the door. He appeared a little breathless, as if he'd been moving furniture—or exercising.

Crying "uncle" was exactly what crossed her mind, except not in the sense of the word that referred to family. She thought of it more in terms of surrender.

Her mother's taste had definitely improved, Jewel thought, covertly taking in Christopher Culhane's features. The man was tall and dark and he made the word *handsome* suddenly turn into a dreadfully inadequate description.

"Can I help you?" Culhane asked patiently, resting his hands on the boy's whisper-thin shoulders as if to anchor him in place.

Don't get me started, Jewel thought. The next moment, she was tamping down her runaway thoughts. She'd learned a long time ago that all that glittered was definitely not gold.

"Actually, I'm here to help you," she told him. When his expression only became more quizzical, she said, "I'm Jewel Parnell." She held out a business card as if to dispel any doubt as to her identity. "You were expecting me."

What he was expecting, Chris thought, was a man. The woman who'd miraculously made his sister's house habitable again had told him about a Jay Parnell. He realized now that she hadn't been using a name, she'd used an initial.

Still, he heard himself asking, "You're the private investigator?"

"I'm the private investigator," Jewel assured him, then added cheerfully, "Would you like references?" This wasn't the first time she'd been on the receiving end of a disbelieving stare.

"Well, actually..."

"Say no more," Jewel assured him. Opening her oversize purse, she took out a bound folder and handed it to him. "These comments are from all my satisfied customers."

Maybe it was the odd frame of mind he found himself in, but her words presented too much of a straight line for him to pass up. "Where are ones from your dissatisfied customers?"

"There aren't any," she informed him with a touch of pride. Her mouth curved ever so slightly as she lifted her chin.

He looked at the folder and then the woman. What did he have to lose, he decided, except for some time? Besides, he welcomed having someone else in the house to talk to besides the boy.

Stepping back, Chris gestured for her to enter. "C'mon in."

Chapter Two

Jewel looked around as she made her way inside. The house appeared neat and clean, but aside from the vase filled with wildflowers in the center of the coffee table—her mother's touch, she'd know it anywhere—the room was devoid of any real personal touches. It struck her as rather sad.

Her own apartment all but shouted: Jewel Parnell lives here! It wouldn't have been home otherwise. There were knickknacks picked up from years of vacations, photographs documenting both her own life and her mother's, beginning from the time she was a little girl. These were the kinds of things that generated warmth and ultimately gave a place personality.

This house looked clean, but there was no detectable warmth. It didn't give off the aura of a house where a child was being raised.

Her mother had deliberately refrained from giving her any details about the case—utterly out of character for the woman—when she'd given her the name and address of her client. The only thing her mother had told her was that the man was trying to locate someone. Her mother had also said that she'd mentioned that she knew someone who specialized in finding people. Mercifully, her mother hadn't added "usually in sleazy hotels." It might be true, but it wasn't anything Jewel really wanted advertised.

The one thing Cecilia Parnell definitely hadn't mentioned was the little boy who was now watching her intently, as if at any given moment, someone were going to ask him to re-create her likeness from memory.

There was a lot going on behind those dark brown eyes, she decided. She'd never given much credence to the phrase "old soul" until just now.

"This is a nice place," Jewel finally commented in order to break the ice.

It was the boy rather than the man who answered her. "Now." When she looked at him, raising one quizzical eyebrow in a silent query, the boy lifted and lowered his shoulders. "Mom didn't like to clean much," he told her protectively. "But I tried to do it for her when I could."

Her heart going out to the boy, she couldn't hold back her questions any longer. "What's your name?"

"Joel," he told her solemnly.

"My name's Jewel. Jewel Parnell," she said, shaking his hand as if he were an adult. "Now that we're not strangers anymore can you tell me how old you are?"

"Five," he told her.

He sounded more like he was twenty-five, she thought.

Jewel turned toward Culhane and asked, "So what can I do for you?"

But again it was the boy who answered. "Uncle Chris wants you to find my dad."

If ever she'd heard a more mournful-sounding voice, Jewel couldn't remember when.

Because the little boy seemed to be a great deal more forthcoming than the man he'd identified as his uncle, she addressed her next question to the boy. "Did your dad suddenly disappear?"

"Only if you think of three years as being 'sudden.'" This time, it was the man who answered.

Jewel took a step back so she could focus on both of them at the same time and let either one field the questions. It would also help her avoid getting a crick in her neck.

"Any particular reason you want to find him now, as opposed to three years ago?"

"My mom said that we were better off that he was gone."

This was like a tennis match, except that the other team was playing doubles to her singles. Moreover, the boy's reply didn't really answer her question. Why now after all this time?

"I see. His mother is your sister-in-law?" she asked, looking at Chris.

"Sister," he corrected.

Okay, he was doing this for his sister. She could understand that. Family members often took over when the affected member was too upset to function. Something had happened recently to change the dynamics and she'd get to that by and by, she promised herself.

"Could I talk to your sister?" she requested, glancing around as if she expected the woman to be standing back in the shadows.

"Not unless you conduct séances as a sideline."

Chris couldn't help the bitter edge that entered his voice. Maybe he couldn't blame Rita for having an aneurysm, but he could blame her for everything that had come before, for not listening when he'd begged and pleaded with her to go into rehab and make an attempt at reclaiming her life. If not for herself, then for her son. At the time, he'd offered to pay not just for the stint in rehab, but for someone to stay with Joel, as well.

All she had to do was get better. But for that to happen, he thought, she would have to have *wanted* to get better. And she didn't. He was certain that, at bottom, Rita didn't think she deserved to be happy.

Damn it, Rita, why did you throw it all away? Why would you do *something like that? You had a son, for God's sake.*

Jewel could all but feel the tension radiating from the man who would be her client if she decided to take the case.

If, she mocked herself. She knew damn well that unless the man turned out to be a direct descendent of Satan or was numbered among the undead, she was going to take his case. She needed the money.

She also needed to get as much information out of him as possible. She didn't believe in privacy when it came to solving a case or in leaving stones unturned. She always made it a point of knowing what she was getting into and how she was going to maneuver through it. Her first case, which involved tailing a cheating spouse, had taught her that. The wife had failed to mention that her husband was a decorated Marine sniper who felt incomplete without his sidearm somewhere within reach. She'd almost gotten her head blown off when he'd seen the flash from her camera and, enraged, had come charging at her.

Given what Culhane had just said about séances, she could only arrive at one conclusion.

"She's—" Jewel was about to say "dead," but because the boy was standing there, she inserted a euphemism. "Passed away?"

Jewel needn't have tiptoed around the issue. The boy confirmed her suspicion. "My mother's dead."

"I see." *Tough little guy,* Jewel thought. "When did this happen?" She looked from Mr. Tall, Dark and Handsome to the sad little human being standing beside him. The question was up for grabs.

"Two days ago," Chris told her. And he was still trying to catch his breath, he added silently.

"And the funeral?" Jewel wanted to know. "When is that?"

Chris suppressed a sigh. He felt as if everything were crashing in on him. Right now, ordinarily, he'd be at his office at the university, which seemed to be under siege half the time he was there. He was always grading papers or working on his latest textbook collaboration, that is, when he wasn't taking appointments with students. He didn't mind helping them, but the ones who sought him out were generally of the female persuasion, all interested in signing up for private tutoring sessions. Some weren't even taking any of his classes.

Still, fending them off was preferable to this situation. Dealing with death and the consequences that arose because of it was something he'd discovered that he was not any good at.

He reminded himself that he had to call back the funeral director. And find someone to conduct the ceremony, he realized. He didn't like feeling overwhelmed like this.

"Day after tomorrow," he told her, although he saw no reason for her question. He was asking her to find his brother-in-law, not his sister.

Pleased, Jewel nodded. "Good, then it's not too late."

He had no idea what she was talking about. Not too late for what? "Excuse me?"

Rather than repeat herself, she pushed forward. "How many obituaries did you run?"

What did that matter? "Again, excuse me?"

"Obituaries," she repeated, enunciating the word more slowly. "Those are stories in the newspaper that are usually put out by the family to notify the general public that—"

He cut her short. "I know what obituaries are," he retorted, then stopped. "Sorry, didn't mean to snap at you," he apologized. "I'm a little out of my element here."

This had to be hard for him. She remembered what it had felt like when she'd lost her father. She and her mother had gotten through it by leaning on each other, as well as their friends. "Isn't there anyone to help you?"

"I'm helping him," Joel piped up solemnly.

She looked down at the boy. "I'm sure you are." She said it without sounding patronizing. From the little she'd picked up, Joel seemed to be a lot more capable than some adults she'd dealt with. "But this is probably all new to you, too," she suggested delicately with a kind smile. "I guess you'll just help each other along." She shifted her eyes back to Culhane. "About the obituaries…?"

Chris shrugged. "There's no point in putting them out." He glanced at Joel and decided to omit the fact that, for the past four years, Rita had predominantly been involved with drug pushers and users, none of whom would come to a funeral, thank God. "From what I gathered, Rita kept to herself a lot the past few years. She didn't have any friends."

Jewel glanced to see how the boy was dealing with that. There was no change in his demeanor, but she thought she noticed an even more stricken look in his eyes.

"This runaway ex-brother-in-law you're looking for, if he lives or works anywhere in the county, he might read the obituary and come to the funeral."

Chris thought about Ray. He'd never met anyone more self-serving and self-involved. "What makes you think he'd come?"

"Any number of reasons," she assured him. "Disbelief. Curiosity. Remorse. You'd be surprised how many different reasons there are for people to come to a funeral. It's not all about paying last respects."

Culhane's expression bordered on dark, she thought.

"You're assuming that he can read," was his bitter comment.

"Or has someone to read to him," she supplied without skipping a beat.

The answer brought the first semblance of what would have passed for a semi-smile to his lips. It seemed, she noted, to soften his entire countenance. It also made him look younger, more approachable.

Why hadn't any of her professors ever looked like that, she wondered.

Her comment made him come around a little, which, in turn, had him realizing that he hadn't even offered her anything. "Hey, I'm sorry, this whole thing has thrown me for a loop. Would you like something to drink?"

"No." A smile played on her lips as she looked toward the living room and the sofa there. "But sitting down might be nice."

Chris felt like an idiot. Despite occasional lapses when he was preoccupied with his work, he wasn't normally this socially awkward.

"The sofa's comfortable," the boy told her with the solemnity of someone delivering a sermon at High Mass on Sunday.

He threaded his small fingers through hers. Here was a boy who'd already learned how to take charge, not because he was pushy, but because he'd had to.

"It's right here," Joel told her, leading her to the sofa.

"Thank you," she said with sincerity, smiling at him

as she sat down. To her surprise, Joel remained standing, as if he wasn't sure he wanted to join her.

Culhane sat down in the love seat that was adjacent to the sofa. "Joel is holding it together better than I am," he confided.

Jewel gave herself a moment to study him more closely. "Were you and your sister close?" she asked sympathetically.

"Once," he recalled. And it felt as if that had been a million years ago, Chris thought. He could hardly remember Rita the way she'd once been. "Before things went spiraling out of control," he said tactfully, glancing at his nephew.

"And when did that start happening?" Jewel wanted to know.

Chris hesitated for a moment, then looked again at Joel. He couldn't speak freely with him around. He had a feeling that the boy was absorbing every word and he didn't want to be responsible for making him feel any worse than he already did.

He pointed toward the family room. "Joel, why don't you go and play a video game?"

The boy remained standing where he was. "I don't have any."

Chris stared at him. That was impossible, he thought. He had specifically sent Rita extra money for the boy's birthday and earmarked part of it for a game console and several of the more popular games. He'd said so in the note he'd included. He would have called if Rita would have taken his call, but after hearing the receiver on the other end being banged down a couple of dozen times, he'd learned his lesson.

"You don't?" he asked incredulously.

Joel shook his head. "No."

"Well, I just happen to have a portable game console in my purse," Jewel announced. Out of the corner of her eye, she saw Culhane looking at her quizzically as she took it out. "It's something I use while I'm doing surveillance." Which happened a lot more frequently than she was happy about. She never liked being inert for long. "That can be deadly dull and playing with this keeps my mind sharp."

She could see that Culhane looked skeptical, but she didn't bother explaining that the console also supported brain teasers and ways to test IQ skills. She wasn't trying to justify having one to him, she just wanted to explain why she had one in her possession.

Joel was looking at her uncertainly. She surrendered the video game player to him. "Okay, now why don't you take that into the family room?" Jewel suggested. "That way, you can play without having us disturb your concentration."

Joel gave her a look that told her he saw through the ruse, but played along anyway.

"I take it that you sent Joel a game console," she asked Chris the moment his nephew was out of earshot.

"I sent my sister money to buy him one," he corrected, then looked at her, slightly mystified. "How did you know?"

She laughed softly. "It wasn't hard to put the pieces together." When he still looked at her doubtfully, she added, "Mostly that surprised look on your face gave it away."

"You looked surprised, too," he pointed out.

She didn't argue. "Moderately so because all the kids I know or have dealt with eat, sleep and breathe video games. You, on the other hand, looked as if something that you took to be a given had just turned out to be wrong. There's a difference."

"Obviously," he commented, then shifted so that he could scrutinize her a little more closely. She was sharp, he'd give her that. Or maybe she was just good at coming off that way. "That's a pretty good card trick."

He was testing her, Jewel thought, maybe trying to see if she were quick to take offense. He was going to be disappointed.

"I don't do card tricks," she countered with an easy smile. "I'm a student of human nature. And I get straight A's most of the time."

She paused for a moment, trying to read him. There were a lot of signals coming off the man. Anger, grief, confusion. All of which were completely understandable, she thought.

Jewel wondered which would win out in the end. Or was this all going on as he tried to come to grips with what had just happened? It had to have changed the dynamics of his world.

"So, do I have the job?" she asked. "Or do you want to reserve judgment on that until you check out my references?" She nodded toward the folder she'd handed him earlier.

He waved away the second part of her words. He was

going on his instincts. Besides, he was in no mood to have to conduct interviews. "You've got the job."

"All right, about the terms—"

Again he waved his hand. "Mrs. Parnell already told me your rates."

"Oh, she did?" She tried very hard not to sound annoyed. Her mother had no business quoting her going rates. Since when did her mother even *know* what her rates were?

He nodded. "She said they were reasonable—and if I didn't think so, to call her and she'd handle it. She said the two of you have a close working relationship. I take it you've done a lot of work for her?"

"In a manner of speaking," Jewel allowed. "She's my mother." He looked somewhat surprised. "Does that make a difference?" she asked.

He thought a moment, then shook his head. "No."

"All right, since that's out of the way, I'm going to need as much information as you can give me."

"About Ray?" he asked.

"About everything," she specified. She thought she saw him clam up. Privacy issues? "Your sister, your missing ex-brother-in-law, your nephew. The first thing I'm going to do is contact the local papers to run that obituary tomorrow. For that, I'm going to need her full name, her date of birth, if there are any other surviving siblings—"

"No."

"Or children—"

"No."

The piece was going to be short and sweet, she

thought. Didn't matter, she'd find a way to dress it up a little.

Jewel took out a digital recorder from her purse. Placing it on the coffee table, she switched it on. "Okay, I don't want you to hold anything back. Tell me everything that comes to your mind when you think of your sister."

The device began recording. It had nothing to work with but silence.

Chapter Three

Jewel raised her eyes. He didn't look like a man who was trying to sort out his thoughts. He looked more like a man who was resigned to remaining silent.

"The recorder works better if it has something to record," she told him gently. "Though it might happen someday in the future, right now, technology hasn't advanced enough so that machines can record a person's thoughts."

This was hard on him. Anger had merged with a porcupine-edged sense of guilt. Would she be alive today if he'd insisted on continuing to come around? If he'd made Rita see a doctor...

Chris blew out a breath. "I don't know what to say," he admitted.

What was it about the sight of a digital recorder that

made so many people, even talkative ones, freeze? Jewel wondered.

"This isn't going to make it into any archives or be preserved for posterity," she promised him. "It's just to help me remember what you said. Again," she prompted gently, "the key word here is *said*." She gave him a starting-off point. "Did you ever actually meet Joel's father?"

Did she think he could amass this kind of animosity through hearsay alone? "Oh, yeah. I met him."

The way he said it told her that he'd disapproved of his sister's husband right from the very beginning. But she still asked her question anyway. "What was your first impression?"

He shrugged, struggling to keep the emotion out of his voice. "For Rita's sake, I wanted to like him. But I saw that he was loser, as well as a user. I knew that somewhere down the line, Rita was going to regret getting involved with him and—"

"Hold that thought," Jewel requested. Much as she really hated doing it—she had a feeling that it was going to be hard to get Culhane started again—she held her hand up to temporarily stop him from continuing.

Jewel felt rather than saw that the boy had drifted back into the room. Turning, she saw him standing in the doorway, holding the portable video game player in his hands. His attention wasn't riveted on the screen, it was on them.

This wasn't anything a boy should hear about his father, Jewel thought. At least, not at this age. Five was very young to have your illusions crushed, no matter how mature you seemed.

Beckoning the boy closer, she smiled at him and asked, "Is there something wrong, Joel?"

The boy crossed to her, holding out the unit she'd given him. He looked chagrinned as he admitted, "I don't know how."

Was it the game that was stumping him? Or was there something else? Was he just casting about for an excuse to come back in? "Don't know how to what?" she asked him kindly.

Joel sighed, thrusting the unit into her hands. It obviously embarrassed him to admit this. "To play with this."

"Don't any of your friends have one of these?" He shook his head. Though she'd asked the question, Jewel found that a little difficult to believe. Did he hang out with Amish kids? "They don't have one of these?" she repeated to make sure she understood what he was telling her.

"No," Joel said in a small voice. "I don't have any friends."

That hadn't occurred to her. He was too young to be a loner. "What about at school? Nobody there that you talk to or like to hang out with?"

There was a blank expression on his face. "I don't go to school."

This time, it was Chris who was caught off guard by what Joel said. He looked at his nephew, stunned. If anyone belonged in a school, to have his potential maximized, it was Joel. "You're kidding."

"Mama said I needed to stay home with her," Joel told him matter-of-factly. "She said she needed me to help her with things."

"What kind of things?" Chris wanted to know. Just how badly had their lives disintegrated? Again he up-braided himself for letting things go the way they had. Why hadn't he made it a point to force Rita to mend fences so that he see for himself what was going on in her life?

The small shoulders moved up and down beneath the washed-out T-shirt. "Breakfast. Lunch. She said she liked the way I washed the clothes," he volunteered, obviously clinging to the offhanded praise.

Jewel could see that the revelation affected Culhane. He was probably struggling with the guilt that all this dredged up. Momentarily putting her interview with him on hold, Jewel shut off the recorder, made eye contact with the boy and patted the place next to her.

"Come sit by me, Joel," she coaxed. Dutifully, he did as he was told, looking somehow even smaller as he sat beside her. "I'm sure your mother really liked having you around and that you were a great help to her, but you do need to go to school. It's important that you learn things, like how to read and—"

"I know how to read," Joel interrupted.

"You do?" She doubted if the boy was capable of lying. "Did your mama teach you?"

Again, Joel shook his head, looking very solemn. "Alakazam taught me," he told her.

The name sounded like something a child would

make up, Chris thought. Was he talking about some imaginary friend? "Who?"

Still maintaining eye contact with Joel, Jewel responded to Culhane's question. "That's the name of a character on a public broadcasting station program. It's one of those shows that's geared to help kids learn basic things, like reading, and adding and subtracting simple numbers. I have a feeling that your sister might have relied on the TV to act as a babysitter for Joel. Thank God for programs like that," she added, smiling at the boy.

Jewel glanced in Chris's direction. "You're going to need to enroll him in school," she told him. The unexpected news brought a frown to his lips. He probably hadn't a clue about things like registration, she thought. Handsome as hell, the man made her think of the absentminded academic. "Your wife handles these kinds of things?" she guessed.

The question seemed to come out of the blue and threw him for a moment. "What? No. I don't have a wife," he added.

"I see." Of course he wasn't married. For a second, she'd forgotten that her mother was the one who had brought them together. It would have been the first thing Cecilia Parnell would have ascertained before she started the wheels turning. "Would you like me to help you get him registered?" she asked. The moment the offer was on the table, Culhane looked incredibly relieved. It was all she could do not to laugh at his expression. "I'll take that as a yes."

Joel fidgeted beside her. When she looked at him, he

appeared far from happy. "What's wrong, honey?" she asked the boy.

"Do I have to go?" he asked sorrowfully.

Rather than impress upon him that it was the law, Jewel tried to make it sound like something that he could look forward to.

"You'll like going to school," she promised. "You get to play games and meet other kids your own age. You'll make friends," she promised.

But he didn't look so sure. Joel's apprehensive expression remained. "What if they don't like me?"

She looked at him as if that were just not possible. "What's not to like?" she asked incredulously. Jewel grinned broadly at him, refraining from tousling his very silky dark hair. "You're a cool guy," she declared. Then, inclining her head as if she was about to share something exclusive, she said, "Let me let you in on a secret. You just talk to them about things they're interested in and they'll like you."

His eyes widened just a little. "Really?"

In an exaggerated motion, she crossed her heart. "Really. I have it on the best authority." And then Jewel nodded at the portable video game player he was still holding in his hands. "Would you like me to show you how to play that?"

The shy expression was back, as was the small, uncertain voice. "Yes, please."

"Love those manners," she commented, then raised her eyes to Chris. "You don't mind, do you? This'll only take a minute." And then she added with another grin, "No extra charge."

It hadn't occurred to Chris to even worry about the cost. He felt far too out of his element with everything else that was going on to worry about being charged for the extra time it might take to show his nephew how to use a video game player.

He urged her on with an absolving wave of his hand. "Go ahead."

She turned her attention back to the boy. "You heard the man. Let's get to it. Now, you have to hold it like this." Jewel demonstrated what she meant, then took Joel's small fingers and arranged them on either side of the game player.

Getting the dexterity part under control took longer than she'd expected, but once that was mastered, Joel caught on very quickly. She had a feeling he would. She had him playing the game in no time, conquering aliens with subdued relish.

Once he was entrenched in the game, rather than send the boy back to the family room to play, Jewel decided that it might be a better idea not to distract him. She motioned for Chris to adjourn to the kitchen with her. That way, they could keep an eye on Joel and she could still conduct the rest of the interview. If she were going to find Ray Johnson, she needed as much information as Culhane could possibly give her.

Sitting down at the table for two, the recorder once again in position, Jewel turned it on for the second time and said, "Now, where were we?"

Instead of trying to recall what he'd said to her, Chris commented, "You're pretty good at this, aren't you?"

"Tracking people down? Actually, I am," she told him.

Not that she'd had all that many missing persons cases, but the few that she'd had, she'd successfully located.

To her surprise, Chris shook his head. "No, I mean talking to kids."

"Oh."

She looked over toward the living room. His nephew was sitting on the sofa, his small face screwed up with concentration as he worked his way from one level to the next with, whether he realized it or not, amazing speed.

Jewel shrugged off his observation carelessly. "They're just short people," she told him. "And I still remember being a kid," she confessed. She had an all-encompassing empathy that served her well in her line of work. "Besides, your nephew seems extremely bright. I think if you have him tested, you'll probably find that he's very gifted. Possibly even a genius."

Chris glanced over toward the boy. "I really hope not," he said with feeling.

She didn't quite follow. She would have thought that someone like him, a college professor, would have been thrilled.

"Why not?" she asked, curious. "Taking tests is a lot easier when you're gifted. Cuts down on hours and hours of cramming," she added, remembering all-night study sessions that still didn't yield the results she'd hoped for. While she had a mind like a sponge when it came to certain things, studying dry subject matter had never come easily to her.

He was still looking at the boy. "If you happen to

be different in any way, people tend to think of you as being strange."

Jewel studied Culhane for a long moment. "Speaking from experience?" she finally guessed.

This wasn't why he was hiring her. He didn't want her delving into his life, he just wanted her to find the boy's father. "What kind of information did you say you needed?"

She saw the "No Trespassing" sign being posted as clearly as if he had pounded it into the ground right in front of her. But if that was the way he wanted it, that was fine with her. She was curious, but it wasn't terminal and besides, everyone deserved to keep his privacy intact.

She checked the recorder to make sure it was on. "Tell me anything you can remember about your sister's husband. Let's start with where he worked. Do you remember the address?"

"He didn't work," Chris corrected her. "At least, not during the years he was with Rita."

She was familiar with the type. "Did he *ever* hold down a job?"

Chris nodded. That was how the whole thing began. "He used to work in a garage. Rita crashed her car and her insurance company sent her to this repair shop they had a contract with for an estimate. That's how she met Ray. He was the one who worked on her car. He got fired a couple of weeks after that." He frowned, remembering. "She thought it was romantic."

"Romantic?" Jewel echoed. She didn't see the connection. Getting fired seemed like it was anything but romantic.

Chris nodded. "He was fired for blowing off his job to hang out with her. She was nineteen and very young for her age."

Unlike her son, Jewel thought. "And that's the extent of Ray's work history?"

Chris shrugged. He knew it wasn't much to go on and it frustrated him. But then, if there'd been a wealth of information, he would have been able to locate Ray himself. "As far as I know."

"Would you happen to remember the name of the garage?" she asked, mentally crossing her fingers.

"No, but I do remember that it was on Fairview and Carson. I dropped her off to pick up her car." He should have done it for her, he thought. If he had gone in her place, then all of this might have never happened and Rita would still be around.

Even if the boy wouldn't have been.

Jotting down the information, Jewel nodded. "That's a start. Do you have a photograph of Ray?" she asked hopefully. "I noticed that there weren't any photographs around."

"When they divorced, Rita burned all his pictures. Said it was part of the healing process." She'd always been a great one for burning pictures once someone was out of her life. Chris imagined that she'd burned the few she had of him when she'd banished him from her life, too.

Jewel surprised him by nodding. "I've heard of that," she said.

Chris laughed shortly, recalling the incident. Rita had already been heavily into drugs and alcohol. And their relationship was on a downward spiral because he tried to get her to stop.

"Rita almost burned the house down," he told her. "Fire department had to come to put out the fire." He knew that for a fact because her homeowner's insurance wouldn't pay to repair the damages, so he covered the expenses out of his own pocket. "Luckily, they caught it in time so it wasn't a complete disaster."

Right now, there was only one thing that Jewel was interested in. "So then there are no photographs left at all?"

"Yeah, actually there is," he said wearily. She looked at him, waiting. "I have one."

"You?" She wouldn't have thought, given how he felt about the man, that he would have a photograph of him.

Chris nodded. "It's a wedding picture," he explained. "She gave it to me and I never got around to tossing it. Rita was in it," he added unnecessarily.

She knew that was the reason he'd kept it. Not because he was sentimental but, quite possibly, it might have been the only photograph of his sister he had in his possession.

"Good thing," Jewel said. "I'll need it as soon as possible."

"No problem," he told her. "I don't live that far from here."

She glanced over to where Joel was sitting. Now that he'd gotten the hang of it, the boy seemed to be completely engrossed in the video game he was playing. She didn't want him to be disturbed so soon.

"Why don't we get a few more of the questions out of the way before you go retrieve that photograph?" she suggested. Not waiting for Chris to answer, she went on to the next question. "Do you know if Ray ever served in the army or if he was employed anywhere that might have kept his prints on file before he married your sister?"

"He was never in the army," Chris told her, "but he was arrested, so his prints have to be on file with the police department."

This man was sounding more and more like a winner. No wonder Culhane's sister had divorced him. She wasn't feeling all that good about looking for Ray, but she supposed, as the boy's father, he had a right to know that Joel's mother had died. And there was always the infinitesimal chance that the man had changed.

"What was the charge?"

"Drunk and disorderly," Chris recited. That had been the beginning of the end of his sister's marriage, he recalled. "Rita called me in the middle of the night and begged me to bail him out."

She could tell that wasn't his automatic reaction to the situation. "And did you?"

He snorted. In his opinion, jail was too good for Ray. "If it was up to me, I would have had them throw away the key."

"You didn't answer my question," she pointed out. Jewel studied him for a moment and had her answer.

He had a soft spot in his heart for his sister. This had to be killing him. "You bailed him out, didn't you?"

Chris shrugged, frustrated. "She was crying. I was afraid she was going to start drinking again. She was pregnant," he explained.

Pausing, Jewel jotted down a few more notes for herself, then looked up at him. "You sure you want me to find this guy?"

He nodded. "I'm sure. If you don't find him, social services is going to take Joel."

Had she missed something? "Maybe I'm being dense here," she said slowly, "but aren't you Joel's uncle?"

Chris knew where she was going with this and it made him uncomfortable to discuss it. "Yes, but I can't raise him."

It was making less sense, not more. "Again, maybe I'm being dense here, but—"

He cut her off. "I don't know the first thing about raising a kid."

"Most first-time parents don't," she countered. "Kids don't come with instruction manuals. I'm told that you're supposed to learn as you go along."

Maybe, but there were more problems than just that. The idea of being responsible for the care and feeding of another human being, for his very welfare, made him uncomfortable. He wasn't prepared for something like that, didn't feel up to it. Look how he'd dropped the ball with Rita.

For the first time since his parents had died, he was glad that they weren't around so they wouldn't have to see this.

"I'm never home," he told the woman with the luminous eyes who was apparently waiting for more. "With all my work at the university, home is just some place I sleep. Occasionally."

She took all this in quietly, trying not to be judgmental. "If you don't mind my asking, exactly what is it that you do for a living?"

"I teach physics at the University of Bedford."

"A noble profession," she commented with a nod. "And that's it?"

"I'm also collaborating with some other professors on a revised physics textbook, and I just had a paper published in a professional journal."

She waited and when he said nothing more, she pointed out, "Physics professors have children."

His eyes went flat. He wasn't hiring her because he wanted to be challenged. "Physics professors usually have wives first."

He sounded irritated, she thought. She'd overstepped. Again.

Jewel held up her hands as if she were pushing back a blanket because the room had suddenly become too warm. "I'm sorry, I didn't mean to sound as if I were trying to talk you into something. It's just that, from the sound of it, Joel's father isn't exactly going to be up for father of the year, especially if he hasn't come around to see his son since he walked out—"

"He hasn't," Chris assured her.

"And you know this for a fact how?"

He glanced toward the living room. He genuinely felt sorry for the boy, but his situation was what it was. He couldn't take Joel in for more than a few days. Maybe a week. It wouldn't be fair to either of them, especially not to his nephew.

"Joel told me."

She looked over toward the boy and caught herself wondering what Joel thought about all this and how he'd react to being reunited with the father who had apparently wanted no part of him.

For the time being, she kept the rest of her thoughts to herself.

But her heart went out to the boy.

Chapter Four

Ray Johnson's features were etched into Jewel's mind as she quietly surveyed the surrounding area in the cemetery, searching for Rita Johnson's errant ex-husband.

It was a sunny Southern California day, but it was atypically muggy. Humidity was rarely a factor in the weather, but every once in a while, it made an appearance just to remind the transplants why they had all migrated here.

There were several other services going on at the same time at the cemetery. Jewel covertly scanned the mourners at each gravesite to see if Ray was there, hanging back so as not to be noticed, watching the woman he had supposedly once loved being buried.

She bit back a frustrated sigh. As far as she could determine, Ray Johnson wasn't anywhere within the vicinity. That wasn't to say that he still might not come.

If he'd read the obituary.

Some people devoured the obituary page, happy to have cheated the Grim Reaper for another day. Others felt it was bad luck to even glance through the obits. Still others were oblivious to its existence.

She supposed it had been a long shot.

Because Chris had been convinced—and rightly so—that Rita's death wouldn't suddenly bring out friends from years gone by who had lost touch with her, and because his sister and the religion she'd been brought up in had had a falling out a long time ago, he saw no reason to go through the charade of a church service. Instead, he asked one of the priests at St. John the Baptist Church to say a few words over Rita's casket before it was lowered into its final resting place. He did it more for Joel than for Rita.

And maybe, Chris allowed, he'd done it a little for himself, as well.

So now, two days after he'd initially hired her, Jewel, Culhane and his nephew were standing at Rita Johnson's gravesite, listening to Father William Gannon offering up prayers and speaking with professional compassion about someone he had never met.

At least, Jewel thought, it had begun with the three of them and the priest. She'd stopped at the deceased woman's house and offered to take both Culhane and his nephew to the cemetery. Culhane had started to demur, saying he was going to drive, but Joel seemed to brighten up a little when he saw her. After a moment of silence, Culhane had thanked her and accepted her offer for a ride to the cemetery.

The priest was just beginning when Jewel saw a woman in black coming up the slight incline, moving quickly despite the fact that her heels were sinking into the grass with each step she took. Leading the way, the woman was followed by two other women, also dressed in black.

The very picture of compassion, Cecilia Parnell came straight to their tight little threesome, her gaze unwaveringly focused on the little boy who stood between his uncle and Jewel.

For one moment, Jewel was almost speechless. She'd thought after all this time that her mother had run out of ways to surprise her.

Obviously, she'd been wrong. "Mother, what are you doing here?" Jewel finally asked.

There was no hesitation on Cecilia's part as she smiled warmly, first at her former client and then at his nephew.

"I'm being supportive of Chris and Joel," Cecilia answered simply. "Worst thing I can possibly imagine is having a loved one die and then adding to that hurt by having no one attend her funeral service," her mother explained.

Jewel supposed she bought that. Sort of. "And Maizie and Theresa?" she asked, nodding at the two women who were just joining them. Theresa looked a little winded.

"They think the same way I do," Cecilia assured her daughter. Turning toward Chris, Cecilia made the introductions before Jewel could. "Chris, Joel," she smiled again at the boy, "these are my very dear best friends, Maizie Sommers and Theresa Manetti."

"Otherwise known as the Greek Chorus," Jewel murmured under her breath. The affectionately voiced remark still earned her a sharp look from her mother.

Each woman shook hands with Chris and expressed her sorrow at his loss. They both included the boy as well, treating him with the same sort of compassion they would have shown to another grieving adult.

Father Gannon cleared his throat. When they looked in his direction, he said, "If I may continue."

"Of course, Father. Forgive the interruption," Theresa apologized for all of them, stepping back beside Maizie.

Rather than stand by her daughter, Cecilia chose to stand on the other side of Chris, the latter and Jewel flanking Joel.

"Anyone else coming?" Father Gannon asked.

Chris raised a quizzical eyebrow in her direction. When she shook her head, he said, "No, no one else."

"All right then," Father Gannon said, and resumed the service.

It was over almost immediately, even though Father Gannon added several more prayers for Rita's soul.

Scanning the outlying area one last time, Jewel glanced down at the boy at her side. It seemed to her that Joel remained amazingly dry-eyed. He hadn't brushed away or shed a single tear from the moment the service began. By contrast, she noticed that her mother sniffled a couple of times into her handkerchief and Theresa was struggling to keep from sobbing. As was Maizie.

All of them, Jewel felt certain, were remembering other, far more personal funerals. Each woman had buried a husband years before she thought she would ever have to. Funerals brought that kind of haunting emptiness back. It was to each woman's credit that she had come out to give a small boy comfort.

Even Culhane, who appeared to have steeled himself against what was going on, had eyes that shone with tears he just barely managed to keep from falling.

Only the boy remained stoic throughout the entire brief ceremony. It was almost eerie, Jewel thought. She was tempted to ask Joel why he wasn't crying, but she refrained.

The service completed, Father Gannon, a large hulk of a man, shyly made his apologies. "I would stay longer, but there is a baptism I must get to."

Chris nodded his head. "A far happier occasion," he agreed as he slipped the priest an envelope with a check for his trouble.

Pocketing the envelope, Father Gannon hesitated a moment longer. He looked from the man to the boy. "If either of you find that you need to talk…" Handing Chris a small card with both his cell number and the church's phone number on it, Father Gannon allowed his voice to trail off.

Chris dutifully pocketed the card without looking at it. It could have been the business card for a local arcade for all he knew.

"Thank you, but that won't be necessary," Chris assured him.

Cecilia backed up his statement by saying, "He and Joel won't be alone, Father."

Jewel gave her a dark look, praying that Culhane

took that as an offer on her mother's part to serve as a compassionate ear. She, on the other hand, knew exactly what her mother meant. She was offering *Jewel's* services. The matchmaker in her mother never died, never rested. Instead, it had gone into overdrive now that Nikki and Kate had "found their soul mates."

As if such a thing really existed.

She'd tailed enough cheating spouses to know that the opposite was far more likely to be true. More than 50 percent of all marriages were doomed from the start. She sincerely prayed that Nikki and Kate would be luckier than most people in their choices.

Father Gannon took his leave and Jewel made a final sweep of the immediate area. The man she was looking for was still nowhere in sight. Either from lack of knowledge, or for some other, more complex reason, Ray Johnson hadn't shown up to pay his last respects to the mother of his son.

Placing his hand on Joel's shoulder to guide the boy out of the cemetery, Chris turned to the trio of older women. "Ladies, I'd like to thank you for coming here today—" He got no further.

"Oh, but we're not leaving you and Joel just yet," Cecilia informed him. There was just the appropriate touch of cheerfulness in her voice. Not so much that it detracted from the solemn occasion, but just enough to indicate that things *did* have a way of getting better.

"I brought food," Theresa volunteered. "We can set it up once we get to your house."

Chris had no idea what to make of these women, two of whom had been complete strangers before today.

There was no reason for them, or for the woman whose cleaning company had worked a miracle on Rita's house, to put themselves out like this. He was nothing to them and neither were Joel or Rita. He liked things that made sense and this didn't.

But there was no denying that, along with the confusion, their actions did generate a measure of warmth within him.

Still, he felt he had to protest, even though he sensed that it was futile. "You really didn't have to go out of your way like this."

Jewel felt obligated to intercede. She'd grown up regarding her mother's two best friends as her aunts and, in a great many ways, they were closer than real family. She also knew the way their minds worked—all of their minds. It was only after she, Nikki and Kate had graduated from high school that she came to realize that these kindly faces hid three very devious minds. Each woman was bound and determined to see her daughter and her friends' daughters blissfully wedded with 2.5 children and a white picket fence—and the sooner the better.

Since Nikki and Kate were now, according to the old-fashioned phrase, "spoken for," Jewel was the only holdout, if she didn't count Theresa's son, Kate's brother. She had secretly hoped that they would focus on Kullen because he was older than she was, but apparently age in male years was not the same as age in female years. Consequently, she had become the target of choice.

Well, not today, Jewel thought stubbornly. *And not here.*

"It's what she does," she told Chris. "Theresa runs

a catering service. And Maizie," she added, nodding toward the most animated of the threesome, "is a Realtor. If you decide, down the line," she added expressly for Joel's sake, "to sell either your house or your sister's, she'd be the one to see. She's very good at what she does." Her eyes swept over the three women. "They all are."

"We didn't come to talk business," Cecilia quickly interjected, as if to blot out the effect of her daughter's words. She looked pointedly at Chris. "We came to help any way we can."

Jewel knew that she meant it. "No use fighting it," she advised her client. "Just let them feed you and fuss over you and Joel a little. Otherwise, they'll stay here until you do. They're very stubborn that way. Trust me, I know."

"Sounds like good advice to me." The edges of his mouth curved ever so slightly.

He did appreciate what Cecilia and the other women were trying to do. And if they came over to the house, that meant that he wouldn't have to be alone with the boy. It had been four days since he'd been summoned to the hospital by the police, four days in which he'd been with the boy and he still had no idea what to say, what to do with Joel or how to behave around him. Women were better at this sort of thing, he thought. Even the private investigator he'd hired was better at forming a connection with his nephew than he was.

Added to that, he had to admit that the lack of any sort of display of grief on the boy's part did disturb him.

"Why don't you ride in my car with me and the other

ladies?" Cecilia suggested, looking down at Joel. "I'm not sure I remember exactly where your house is. I need someone to give me directions. Can you do that for me, Joel?"

Joel took his cue like a pro and nodded his head. "Okay."

It was a ruse, Jewel thought, suppressing her annoyance. Her mother was deliberately arranging it so that she and Culhane wound up alone in her car. Her mother didn't need directions, she had a natural, uncanny sense of direction. In addition to which, she also had a GPS mounted on her dashboard that provided alternate routes in case of any traffic snarls or whimsical acts of God and/or nature.

But Jewel knew that she couldn't very well come out and say that. Especially after her mother had successfully convinced Joel to switch vehicles.

It's a car, Mom, not a deserted island. Being alone with the man for ten minutes isn't going to make him want to live happily ever after with me. Or me with him. Especially since there is no such thing.

But she wouldn't mind sleeping with the man, she realized as she stole a glance at the broad shoulders and chiseled, square chin. *After* she located his brother-in-law and closed the case, she silently emphasized.

Squaring her own shoulders, Jewel led the way to her car.

She marched like a soldier, Chris noted, aware of the cadence of her footsteps. He caught himself wondering about her, some of his curiosity, he silently admitted, raised because of the appearance of the other women.

His had been a family in turmoil, more dedicated to shouting at one another and slamming doors to show their displeasure. His parents, he knew, were good people. They just weren't good parents. He supposed he should count himself lucky that he'd turned out the way he had. But why him and not Rita?

Why couldn't he have helped Rita?

At the very least, he should have stopped her from marrying Ray, a move that was, in his eyes, the beginning of the end for her.

Buckling up, Chris glanced at the private investigator he was counting on to help him reclaim his orderly life. He waited until she'd pulled out of the parking space and was weaving her way onto the main road before he said anything. "He wasn't there."

Jewel didn't have to ask. She knew Culhane was referring to his ex-brother-in-law. "Not that I could see, no."

Impatience foiled his ability to stifle a sigh. "Now what?"

Jewel was watching her mother, who was up ahead. After all these years, the woman still drove with a lead foot. You'd think that she would have learned to slow down a bit, be more careful. People complained about older drivers behaving as if they had molasses in their veins. Her mother drove as if she were in training for the Indy 500.

"Now I'll see if I can find out anything from his former employer at that garage you mentioned, the one where your sister first met her ex. Who knows? Maybe the guy stayed in touch with Ray, or gave him a referral when he went looking for another job."

"Another job?" His tone told her he thought that was reaching.

"Man's gotta eat and pay his bills."

Ray had probably found another woman to take advantage of. That was what he was good at. Survival— and falling through the cracks. "And if that doesn't pan out?"

"There are other ways to go," she assured him, deliberately keeping her words vague.

She half expected him to ask her to elaborate. When he didn't, she took a split second to glance in his direction. He was clearly preoccupied. It didn't take much to guess at what was on his mind. She'd seen him watching Joel at the service and the cemetery. The boy's behavior mystified him.

She could see it in their brief interaction at the cemetery. "Don't worry about it."

It took a second for her words to penetrate. When they did, he had no idea what she was referring to. "What?"

"I said don't worry about it," Jewel repeated. "Everyone deals with grief in his own way." She took a guess. "Maybe it's still not real to Joel. Maybe he still believes his mother will walk through the door." She shrugged. "Or maybe he thinks that it's not manly to cry." She glanced at him again just before she made a right turn. "You didn't cry," she reminded him quietly.

She noticed that Culhane squared his shoulders. Was

he being defensive, or had she struck a raw nerve? "I don't believe in displaying emotions in public."

Although part of her wanted to explore that a bit further, Jewel let it drop. "Maybe Joel feels the same way."

"He's five," Chris pointed out, emphasizing his age.

That had nothing to do with it. "And he's looking to the only male role model he has."

"Me?" Chris asked incredulously. They'd only been together for four days. People didn't form attachments in four days.

But, obviously, his private investigator saw it differently. "You," Jewel confirmed.

Chris snorted. "You're wrong. The last time I saw Joel, he was two years old. How can I be his role model? He has no memory of me."

"Maybe, maybe not. I can remember something that my mother tells me happened when I was only eighteen months old."

Now she was just making things up. If this was the way her mind worked, maybe he'd been a little too hasty in hiring her. "That's not possible."

"The brain is a very strange organ," Jewel informed him. She pressed down on the accelerator. Her mother was pulling farther and farther away. "Everything that's ever happened to us, every song we've heard, everything we've ever seen, is imprinted there somewhere." She shouldn't have to be telling him this. "You're a scientist, you should know that."

"Not exactly my field of expertise," he countered. Chris took a breath, reconsidering her argument. It seemed almost impossible. "So you think he's trying to imitate me?"

"He's trying to be a man, and you're the closest role model he has. You heard him—he has no friends. Consequently, there are no fathers in his life, no one to take cues from." She smiled, turning down another block. "Until you came along."

"Four days ago," he emphasized again.

"The length of time doesn't matter," she insisted. "You saw him. You're here now and he absorbs things like a sponge."

"So you're telling me that if I cry, then Joel will cry?"

His was the voice of disbelief, she thought. You could lead a horse to water, but getting him to drink was a completely different matter. "Maybe."

"Well, I'm not crying," he told her firmly. He couldn't. If he let his guard down for one second, if he started to remember...

There was nothing to be gained from that, he silently insisted.

"No one's telling you to."

The hell she wasn't, he thought. "Rita knew what she was doing. Knew that she was throwing her life away. Turning her back on her education, on everything our parents wanted for her—" That was probably part of the reason she'd turned her back on it, he thought.

The mention of the senior pair brought up more questions in Jewel's mind. "Where are your parents?"

"They're dead," he said matter-of-factly. "My father was literally hit by a Mack truck and I think my mother just died of a broken heart six months later. She felt as if she had nothing to live for. They argued a lot, but they loved each other."

That didn't make any sense to her. Her mother had been distressed when her father had died, but she never lost her focus as a mother.

"But Rita was still alive," Jewel argued.

He lifted a shoulder in a vague half shrug. "In a manner of speaking. I wasn't the only one Rita cut ties with. She didn't like to have to sit through lectures."

Who did? Jewel thought. "I'm sorry."

The last thing he wanted was pity. "There's no reason for you to be sorry," he told her.

She looked at him for a long moment. They'd arrived at his late sister's house and she still had to park, but this took precedence over that. "If you think that," she told him, "then I'm even sorrier."

Chapter Five

The moment Maizie, Theresa and Cecilia walked into the house that had known very little laughter and joy in the past several years, the three women did what had come naturally to them all their lives: they took control.

As Jewel stood back and watched, these powerhouses in three-inch heels took charge not just of the space, but of the boy and his uncle, as well.

Resistance is futile, she thought with barely hidden amusement. She wondered if either, especially Culhane, knew that they never stood a ghost of a chance. Deceptively petite and innocent looks to the contrary, the ladies were formidable forces to be reckoned with. She knew that firsthand.

While Theresa served the food she'd prepared for the occasion, Jewel saw her mother moving about, straightening whatever had somehow gotten out of place since the last time she had been here. That left Maizie to entertain Joel, something she did with aplomb. The fact that Nikki's mother had been a grandmother-in-training from the moment her daughter had graduated from medical school certainly didn't hurt.

That left Jewel with Culhane.

Just the way she knew her mother and the two women her mother had shared her innermost secrets with since the third grade wanted it.

Too bad this isn't going to go anywhere, ladies, she thought. The man was charmingly unaware of his seductive sensuality, which was an excellent—not to mention rare—quality, but she got the impression that he wasn't in the market for a relationship, and God knew that she wasn't. A memorable night of torrid sex, sure, but a lasting relationship? That was like pursuing a unicorn. It was a mythical thing that didn't exist except in fairy tales and dreams.

"This really isn't necessary," Chris was protesting again as Theresa handed him a plate of food she'd just put together.

Behind the women were an array of casserole dishes and warming trays filled to capacity, which might easily have fed a small village if the occasion arose. Theresa had never believed that the words *food* and *moderation* belonged in the same sentence. Or the same room.

"Don't protest," Jewel advised, accepting her own plate from Kate's mother. "It won't do you any good and besides, it keeps them busy and off the streets."

She glanced about the room, now so neat it almost

hurt. Maizie was cheering Joel on as he played his video game—Jewel had insisted that he keep hers so that he could practice. And because she had run out of things to tidy, her mother was now rinsing off the serving spoons despite the fact that they all knew they were going to be used again almost immediately.

"Somewhere," Jewel commented with a shake of her head, "Donna Reed is looking down and smiling."

Her mother's eyes narrowed as Cecilia focused in on her. "There's nothing wrong with dusting off old-fashioned skills, Jewel. Sometimes a person just needs a break from the fast-paced modern world." Cecilia turned toward Chris for backup. The narrowed eyes were gone, replaced with a wide, warm smile. "Don't you agree, Chris?"

Engrossed in the process of having a piece of prime rib melt away on his tongue, Chris was momentarily distracted. When he saw Cecilia looking at him, he realized that she'd asked him a question and he had missed it completely. "Excuse me?"

Jewel came to his rescue. He might be a learned college professor, but he wasn't a match for a card-carrying member of the triumvirate.

"Mom, he's just taken a bite of Theresa's prime rib. The man'll agree to anything," Jewel pointed out. She grinned at Chris, waving him on. "Never mind, just eat. My mother was just advancing one of her favorite theories."

Over in the corner, their eyes on the small screen in the boy's hands, both Maizie and Joel suddenly cheered.

Joel had defeated the alien force and made the world safe for humanity once again.

Maizie was the louder of the two.

"This is a very sharp young man," Maizie announced, congratulating Chris. She looked at her companion. "What grade did you say you were in? Because I think you'll be ready for high school the day after tomorrow."

"I'm not in a grade," Joel told her simply.

"You're not?" Maizie asked incredulously. She looked at him, confused. "How's that possible?"

"Because I'm not in school," Joel answered. There was a touch of self-consciousness to his reply, as if he now realized that this wasn't right.

There was a skeptical expression on Maizie's face when she looked over toward Jewel and the boy's uncle. "He's not in school?"

"No," Jewel answered before Chris could. She didn't want the man being badgered, and whether they knew it or not, the triumvirate had a tendency to badger. "But that's being handled."

Maizie looked relieved. "You've enrolled him?" she asked Chris.

"Not yet," he admitted.

"Has he had his—inoculations?" Maizie changed terms at the last moment. Because her daughter was a pediatrician, Maizie was more up than most on certain requirements that school-aged children had to meet before they were even allowed to register.

But Joel was not content to let the world roll right over

him. He had questions. Especially when things pertained to him. "What's in-noc-ulations?" he wanted to know.

Jewel sensed that sugarcoating it would only earn his distrust once he found out what the word meant. So she gave him the truth.

"Shots," she told him despite her mother waving her hand behind the boy's back to make her stop. "You go to the doctor and he or she gives them to you to keep you healthy."

Instead of displaying fear, the way Maizie and the other women clearly anticipated, the boy merely shook his head. "Not me."

She made a guess as to his meaning. "You've never had a shot?"

Joel shook his head again, his bangs sweeping back and forth across his forehead from the force of his denial. "I never went to the doctor."

"You must have been one very healthy boy," Cecilia commented in surprise.

Joel shrugged, as if he really didn't know if that was the case, one way or another. "Mama said I could get well by myself."

The three older women exchanged looks tinged with sadness that there were mothers out there who were only focused on themselves and consequently hardly paid the least attention when it came to their children's welfare.

However, it was Chris who voiced their collective concern out loud. He couldn't believe what he was hearing. "Your mom *never* took you to a doctor?"

Joel looked as if he didn't understand what all the

fuss was about. He'd never known any other life but the one he'd led, causing him to believe that this was how things were done.

"No."

Chris could feel his temper rising. Apparently, the loving, caring sister he'd known had died not the other day but a very long time ago.

"Ever?" he pressed.

"No." Joel fidgeted, sensing his uncle's barely contained displeasure. "Don't get mad at her, Uncle Chris. I was okay," he insisted.

"He's not mad, honey." Standing up, Jewel crossed to the boy and put her arm around his shoulders. "He's just concerned about you, that's all."

"I can call Nikki," Maizie volunteered. "I think she can find out if Joel's ever received any of his required immunizations. There's some database or something they can access for that," she explained with a careless wave of her hand. "I'm sure she can see him tomorrow," the woman added brightly.

"Who's Nikki?" Chris wanted to know.

"Maizie's daughter," Theresa volunteered.

"And an excellent pediatrician," Maizie interjected with pride.

"Tomorrow's Saturday," Jewel pointed out. They probably wouldn't be able to get things moving until Monday.

But Maizie was undaunted. "Doesn't matter. Nikki'll see him," she promised with confidence. "She owes me. I gave her life. I'll call her and let her know what's up so she can get started," Maizie said, taking out her cell phone.

Because she sensed his bewilderment, Jewel looked over toward Chris. She was right. He was wearing a mystified expression. The threesome took a lot of getting used to once they got going. They certainly could be overwhelming at times.

Her eyes met his. "They all think like this," she explained. "It comes naturally to them. They're über-mothers to the nth degree."

He glanced in Joel's direction. Now it was the woman who had brought all the food—Theresa he thought her name was—who was fussing over the boy. And the poor kid was lapping it up like some flower someone forgot to water for a very long time.

Chris's heart went out to the boy. "Über-mother," he repeated almost to himself. "That's not such a bad thing."

She could only laugh and shake her head. The man was a newbie. "You say that now. Try living with it for a while, *then* come back to me."

Belatedly, Jewel realized how the last part of her sentence sounded—as if it were an open invitation to Culhane, or at least an assumption that they were going to have an ongoing relationship rather than just a one-time client-investigator interaction. That was *not* what she was trying to convey.

Because she didn't know how to backtrack gracefully without being obvious or sticking her other foot in her mouth, Jewel took the only option that was left to her— she changed the subject.

"Maizie's daughter is a great pediatrician. If anyone can get Joel's chart up-to-date, she can," she promised Chris enthusiastically. "That way, there'll be no problem getting him registered for school. You can have him in a kindergarten class in a week, if not less," she concluded.

Chris looked from Jewel to the triumvirate and then back again. "Which one?" he wanted to know. His world revolved around the university. He hadn't a clue when it came to elementary schools in the area. "Which school do I take him to?"

The question sounded deceptively simple. At first. "The one closest to the house," Jewel told him. "Maizie is very good at knowing which neighborhood is in what school district." The information she was giving him didn't seem to enlighten Chris. The thoughtful frown remained and deepened just a little. "What's wrong?"

The woman was missing a very basic point, he thought. "If you don't find Ray in the next few days, which address do we use for Joel?"

To her, that was a minor point. There weren't *that* many elementary schools in Bedford. It was a very desirable place to live, but in comparison to many of the surrounding cities, it was still in its infancy. "Didn't you say you lived nearby?"

"Not all that nearby," Chris confessed.

And he had no idea if his house and his late sister's were even in the same school district. He had a feeling that they probably weren't. Nothing was ever simple when it came to Rita, he thought.

He lowered his voice, as if to spare Joel from hearing

this. But the boy had stopped what he was doing and placed the handheld console on the coffee table. He was very aware that he had become the topic of conversation and was intently listening to his fate being bandied about.

"Staying here for a few days to help Joel deal with this situation is one thing," Chris was saying, "but all my reference books, my notes for my research, all that's over at my house."

Jewel didn't see any of this as a problem. The situation was fluid. The main thing was to get the boy into a school where he could take his first steps toward a formal education.

"All right, why don't you use that as Joel's address for the time being?" she suggested, then flashed the boy an encouraging smile. "When I locate his father, things can be adjusted."

She'd counted on support from her mother and the other two women. She'd forgotten how unpredictable they could be.

"Uprooting the boy so much won't be good for him," Theresa said quietly.

Jewel was about to protest that it wouldn't be for that long, but Chris had already turned toward the woman and asked, "What do you suggest?"

"Since your intent is to find the boy's father, and he'll likely move back in, why don't you use this house as an address?" Cecilia suggested.

Drawn into the discussion, Maizie temporarily shut her cell phone as she raised another point. "What if Jewel can't find his father?"

Cecilia frowned at the mere suggestion that could happen. "Jewel could find an angel's shadow if she had to."

"Luckily, I don't have to," Jewel murmured under her breath, then turned toward Chris, covering her embarrassment with a quip. "My mother's just the tiniest bit prejudiced."

Rather than agree, or laugh, Chris surprised her by saying, "Hey, enjoy it while you have it." It earned him the approval not only of Theresa, but of all three of the women. Despite their thriving careers, all three were first and foremost mothers.

Cecilia beamed and patted Chris on the shoulder. "I knew I liked this young man the minute I saw him."

But Maizie had another wrench to throw into the plans. "What if Jewel finds him and he doesn't want to move back into this house? What if the man wants to take Joel to live with him instead of the other way around? He's got to be living somewhere," she pointed out.

This was getting out of control, Jewel thought. She held up her hands as if to physically stem the flow of words.

"Stop, stop," she pleaded. When the growing noise level died down, she addressed her suggestion not to any of the three women, but to Chris. After all, the decision, no matter how long they debated it, was ultimately his. "For now, why don't we just register Joel in this school district? That way, he can meet some of the kids in the neighborhood. If things change, we'll deal with them then."

She realized her mistake the minute the words were out. She'd said *we*.

She'd just injected herself into the mix. While she did work closely with any clients she took on and checked in with them regularly, once a case was over, so, for the most part, was the contact. In this particular case, she didn't want to inadvertently make her mother think that there was any sort of a match being struck here in the long run—or even the short run.

"I mean, *they'll* deal with them then," she deliberately corrected herself. She avoided looking at Culhane, afraid of what she might see in his eyes. Amusement, surprise or apprehension—none of it was something she would have moved into the "win" column.

It was Maizie who finally broke the silence and gave Jewel's idea the seal of approval.

"Sounds like a plan to me," she agreed. Holding up her still-dormant cell phone, she said, "I'll make that phone call now." There was a sliver of a question in her voice as she once again opened up the phone. She glanced at Chris to see if he concurred.

Feeling somewhat at loose ends, he nodded.

Maizie moved toward the kitchen, punching in the numbers that would connect her directly to her daughter no matter where she was.

Looking bewildered, Joel tugged on the hem of Jewel's blouse. "What's happening?"

He'd gotten overwhelmed, she thought. *Welcome to the club, kid.* It took effort not to get lost in the verbal back-and-forth pitches.

"Well, it looks like the short of it is we'll be getting you some friends," she told him.

Because that would be where, hopefully, this project

would end: with his enrolling in kindergarten and making friends with at least a few children in the class. To her, that was more important than what address he used.

Her words did not get the reaction she'd hoped for. Joel looked upset. "I don't need any friends," he told her.

"Everyone needs friends," she told him kindly.

Jewel knew that the boy was probably afraid, and she could understand that. Being the "new kid" anywhere was an uncomfortable feeling. It was worse when you were a kid—even a brilliant kid.

As she made her pronouncement, she couldn't help glancing in Chris's direction. She had a feeling that, despite his kneecap-melting good looks, Christopher Culhane was a bit of a loner himself.

"Hey, wait, I *do* have friends," Joel told her suddenly.

This was a complete 180-degree change from a couple of minutes ago. She didn't picture the boy as someone who would deliberately tell a lie—especially one that was so blatant and easily disproved.

"You do? Who?" she wanted to know.

Joel never hesitated. Instead, he looked very solemn as he made the revelation. "You. And the nice ladies here."

Damn, but he was good, she thought. This time, she gave in and affectionately ran her fingers through his hair. She was pleased that he didn't flinch or pull back. "That's very sweet, Joel, but we're all adults, honey."

That response only confused him. "I can only be friends with kids?"

She knew that sounded way too confining to him.

Plus she had a feeling that, given his maturity level, Joel was probably currently stuck somewhere between the world of adults and the world of children. An unfortunate outsider to both. He was most likely safer among adults. They might ignore him or dismiss him, the way his mother probably had, but at least adults wouldn't ridicule him the way kids did with someone who was different.

Still, the longer that was put off, the harder it would be for Joel to blend in, even a little.

"Of course not," Chris told him firmly. "You can be friends with adults."

The way the man said it reaffirmed her suspicions that he had experienced the same sort of situation when he was Joel's age.

"Your uncle's right. You can be friends with anyone you want," she assured the boy.

Joel's eyes met hers. "So you're my friend?"

She saw that Chris was about to say something that would relieve her of this responsibility, but she answered faster.

"You betcha." She flashed him a grin and put her arm around the slight shoulders. "I'd be honored to be your friend, Joel."

She was rewarded with a bright, sunny smile.

"It's all set," Maizie announced as she shut her cell phone and crossed back to the others. Her eyes swept over both Chris and Jewel. "Nikki can see Joel in her office tomorrow morning at ten. She'll give him a physical and any immunizations that he hasn't had yet."

The boy's bright, sunny smile faded.

Chapter Six

Jewel had no intentions of accompanying Chris and his nephew to Nikki's office. She didn't want either of them, especially Chris, to feel as if she were pushing her way into their inner space. But just as she was about to leave her apartment that morning to attempt to track down Ray Johnson's former employer, her cell phone rang.

Putting down her keys, she fished her phone out of her pocket and glanced at the caller ID. It said "Private," which meant that it could have been anyone. The wide field ran from her mother's landline all the way to various political volunteers begging for contributions in order to keep their party strong.

Though the temptation to ignore the call was great, given her line of work, Jewel really didn't have that luxury. You never knew when another client might be calling—or an anonymous tip might be coming in. She already had several feelers out regarding her present case.

The first thing that had come to her attention was that there were over 653 Ray Johnsons in the country, with more than 220 of them in California. And those were only the ones who were listed. She was sure the number was at least double that amount.

But only one of them was Joel's father.

She had her work cut out for her.

Suppressing a sigh, Jewel flipped her phone open. "Hello?"

"Jewel?" A deep male voice rumbled against her ear. She realized that her hold on the phone had tightened in response. "This is Christopher Culhane. I hate bothering you…"

Ah, if you only knew… The man bothered her in ways he undoubtedly didn't suspect, but she wasn't about to let him know that.

Instead, she cheerfully reminded him, "You're the client, which means that you're paying for the privilege of bothering me anytime you need to." Maybe he'd remembered something that would help her locate his ex-brother-in-law. "So, what can I do for you?"

His answer had nothing to do with finding Ray. "Joel says he doesn't want to go to the doctor."

He'd struck her as a man who was in control of the situation—as long as the situation involved adults. This was something else again. He hadn't a clue when it came to dealing with someone under five feet tall.

Okay, she could be sympathetic, Jewel thought.

"Kids usually don't," she told him. There was a pause

on the other end of the line. A very pregnant pause. Like he was trying to find the right way to ask and not be blunt. Taking pity on him, she decided to bail him out. "Would you like me to go with you? I could meet you at Nikki's office."

The relief she heard in the man's voice told her she'd guessed right. But apparently he still had a problem.

"I'm not sure he'll believe me if I tell him you'll be there." He lowered his voice, leading her to assume that Joel was within earshot. "I get the feeling that my sister broke most of her promises to him. He's not overly trusting."

Once shattered, trust was a hard thing to rebuild. If the most important person in his life didn't keep her word, how could he think that anyone else would? She could see where the boy was coming from, even as she sympathized with Chris's problem.

"Put Joel on the phone, Chris," she requested. "I'll talk to him." The next moment, she heard the sounds of the phone being shifted and handed over.

"Hello?" a small voice said hesitantly.

She kept her own voice cheery. "Hi, Joel. It's Jewel. What's this I hear about you not wanting to go to the doctor this morning?"

"I'm okay, Jewel," the boy insisted. "I don't need a doctor."

Poor kid. He probably thinks he's going to be tortured. "We talked about this, remember? You need to get certain shots before you can go to school. It's to keep you from catching some pretty nasty stuff."

Joel had a counterargument. "I won't catch anything if I don't go to school."

That was fast. "And waste that brilliant lawyerlike mind of yours? No way. C'mon, Joel," she coaxed. "Don't tell me a big, strong guy like you is afraid of an itty, bitty needle."

"I'm not afraid of a needle," he told her with feeling. "I'm afraid of having it stuck into me."

Wow, she thought. *This kid could be president by the time he's twelve.* Jewel looked at her watch. It was getting late. According to Maizie, Nikki had said she'd meet the boy and his uncle at her office at ten. They needed to hit the road. Soon.

"Tell you what. I'll be by in a few minutes and take you and your uncle Chris to the doctor. Dr. Connors is coming in just for you, Joel," she reminded the boy, thinking of the manners he'd displayed. She played on that. "It wouldn't be nice if you didn't show up. You don't want her to come all that way on a Saturday for no reason, do you?"

She heard the boy's deep sigh. "No, ma'am."

"Atta boy," she declared, grinning. "I'll be right there."

Joel and Chris were waiting for her in the driveway when she pulled up. Chris definitely looked relieved and the moment he saw her, Joel's face lit up like a decked-out Christmas tree.

It didn't take much for her to realize that although he might have needed a male role model, the boy was simply starved for female attention. That was one of the reasons he'd responded so well to her mother and her mother's friends. With his own mother gone, Joel had no one to fill that emptiness and he was at loose ends.

If she was given to thinking with her head instead of her heart in situations like this, she would have wondered if perhaps she was doing more harm than good, interfering with the potential bonding process between Joel and his uncle.

But all she knew was that when the little boy's face lit up like that just because he saw her, something reacted inside her in response, a warmth that spread all through her.

She knew her mother would have had some comment about that being her biological alarm clock going off, but she knew it couldn't be that. She liked kids but she'd never experienced that overwhelming desire to have any of her own. Or a husband for that matter.

It was only human to respond to someone who looked that happy to see you, she silently argued. There was no ticking clock involved.

"Hi!" Joel cried, running up to the car, his dark eyes dancing.

"Hi, yourself," she laughed as he opened the door and scrambled into the backseat.

A child his size was supposed to ride in the rear passenger seat, but she was surprised that Joel hadn't tried to sit up front with her. The little boy's capacity for self-discipline, not to mention the extent of the things he seemed to know, just kept on surprising her.

"Sorry to put you out like this," Chris apologized as he got in on the front passenger side.

"Just all part of the service," she assured him cheerfully.

"Really?" he asked. Since he'd never had the need to hire a private investigator before, he had no idea what the job description actually entailed.

Her grin told him that she was kidding. It also, he became aware, evoked an entirely different response from him than he was prepared for. He forced his mind to focus on the business at hand: getting his nephew to the pediatrician for his immunizations.

"I'm making this up as I go along," Jewel admitted. "But so far, it seems to be working out," she told him. Her foot still on the brake, she turned to look in the backseat. "All buckled up?" she asked Joel.

"Yes, ma'am."

She nodded her approval, then glanced to her right. "You, too, Uncle Chris. We're not moving until you have your seat belt on."

It had completely slipped his mind. As he reached for the seat belt, he realized that he was reaching in the wrong direction. Switching hands, he tugged on the seat belt until it was secured around him.

"Not used to riding shotgun?" she guessed, hiding her amusement.

"What?" The term caught him off guard for a moment. "Oh, no, no I'm not. I'm usually driving," Chris explained.

"Would it make you feel more comfortable if you drove to the doctor's office?" Foot still on the brake, she lifted her hands from the wheel to indicate that she didn't mind letting him take over.

It was on the tip of his tongue to say yes, but then, because she'd offered, Chris refrained. He didn't want her to think that he was one of those macho types who needed to pound his chest every fifteen minutes or so just to prove how virile he was. Why he should care what she thought of him was something that he didn't pause to explore. Things were complicated enough already.

"No, that's okay," he told her. "I'm fine with you driving. Besides, you're the one who knows the way."

They weren't exactly traveling to a secret lair, she thought, pressing her lips together to suppress an amused grin. "It's the medical building in Fashion Island."

To her surprise, Chris shook his head. "Afraid I'm not familiar with the area."

It hadn't occurred to Jewel that *anyone* who lived in Southern California was unfamiliar with Fashion Island in Newport Beach. It had been around for *years*. Each year at Christmastime, the merchants outdid themselves when it came to decorating, trying to top the year before. She could remember her parents bringing her there to see it all when she was a little girl. It had become a tradition that she and her mother continued even after her father had passed away. She was extremely sentimental about the area.

"Were you born here?" she asked, curious.

"Here?" Chris echoed.

"In Southern California," she elaborated.

He realized what she was getting at. He didn't get around much. His work ate up his time. "I'm a native," he told her. "But I'm afraid I never had much time for malls and those kinds of places."

She found that almost impossible to believe. "Even as a kid?"

"Especially as a kid," he countered with a dry laugh. He tried to picture his parents chauffeuring him, as he heard that parents did these days with their kids. He drew a blank. "I had no way to get there."

She was about to say that his parents were supposed to be the ones who brought him to the mall as a kid, but the point he was making penetrated. She was beginning to understand why his late sister had such poor self-esteem. And why she hadn't been that much of a mother herself. Rita Johnson lacked role models. Chris and Rita's parents obviously never spent much time with them.

It made her wonder why some people ever became parents at all. It wasn't as if there were no birth control available, or, barring that, no adoption agencies eager to place healthy babies.

Not wanting to press the issue, or possibly open up old wounds, she deliberately changed the subject and looked fleetingly over her shoulder at Joel. Apparently lost in thought, his expression was pensive.

"You'll like Dr. Nikki," she assured him. "She's one of my two very best friends, and she just loves kids."

Joel pressed his lips together grimly and barely nodded. His eyes were wide as he looked around, taking in the scenery. They were traveling down MacArthur Boulevard. The road ahead dipped down, allowing drivers to see the Pacific Ocean in the distance. It was a cloudless, sparkling morning and Catalina, looking like a whale sunning itself, was clearly visible.

Jewel made a left into a parking lot. They had arrived.

Unlike weekdays at this time, there were an infinite number of parking spaces for her to choose from. Only a handful of cars were in the lot, belonging to either physicians or dentists who kept Saturday hours and their patients.

Getting out of the vehicle, Jewel opened the rear door on Joel's side. "Ready?"

Taking a deep breath, and then another when the first one didn't seem to help, Joel nodded. He looked like someone about to walk to his own execution.

"Ready," he said in a voice that squeaked.

Jewel pretended not to notice as she put her hand out to him. "Then let's go and get this over with," she said cheerfully.

"Over with," Joel echoed, nodding vigorously.

Instead of walking abreast of them, Chris fell back and brought up the rear.

She looked natural with his nephew, he thought. Maybe, if his ex-brother-in-law continued to be missing after, say, a month, some kind of an arrangement could be made with this woman to look after the boy. Given the way she got along with Joel, maybe she might even consider becoming his guardian. As he observed the two of them, it was obvious to him that Joel seemed to be a lot happier and more open around Jewel than around him.

Which was fine, Chris silently argued as they got on the elevator. He could see why Joel liked her. She was effervescent, bubbly, while he…well, he was more like orange juice. Healthy, stable, but definitely not bubbly.

Because there was no one else to get on or off, the elevator came to its destination almost a second after they'd gotten on.

"Follow me," Jewel said, and she led the way to the doctor's office.

Not much of a hardship there, Chris thought.

Nikki opened the door herself when Jewel knocked. The honey-blonde looked from Jewel to the two people with her. She nodded a greeting at Chris, but her attention was focused on the small boy standing beside him.

Nikki's bright, electric smile materialized the moment she made eye contact with Joel. "This must be my new patient," she said warmly. Placing one hand on his shoulder, she ushered him in. "I've heard good things about you, Joel."

"You have?" he asked incredulously, his eyes wide.

"I have," she confirmed. "Why don't you and I and your uncle step into Exam Room 1 and we can get all this technical stuff out of the way. After that, if you'd like to ask me some questions, or just talk, I'm all yours."

"Can Jewel come, too?" Joel wanted to know. It was then that Nikki noticed the boy was still clutching on to Jewel's hand tightly.

"I think we might have enough room for her," Nikki answered with a smile. "Let's go in and find out." Turning, she led the way through the empty waiting room to the door that admitted them into the exam area.

"Your friend's just like you," Chris commented, lowering his head to Jewel's ear as he walked behind all of them.

Jewel was fairly certain that he didn't realize it, but when he spoke just now, his breath feathered along the side of her neck. It instantly created a warm shiver up and down her spine, which took considerable effort to stifle. At least from being outwardly visible.

Inwardly was a different matter. It spread its tentacles all through her, leaving no part of her unaffected.

It had been a long while in between men, she thought. Though she told herself that all she was after was earth-shaking, mind-blowing sex, down deep she knew she still had to feel something—respect, admiration, a more than passing attraction, *something*—for the men she went to bed with.

For one reason or another, it had been a long time since she'd "felt" anything at all.

That certainly wasn't the case now.

Jewel cleared her throat before responding. "I take that as a compliment," she told Chris. The man would never know how much effort it took to sound so nonchalant and unaffected, she thought, quietly congratulating herself.

"Well, you passed with flying colors," Jewel told the boy some forty-five minutes later when the three of them were walking out of the eight-story building. "See, I told you that you would."

Glancing down at Joel, she saw the way the boy was looking at his left arm, the site of his inoculations. His expression seemed to indicate that he was deciding whether or not it hurt. He needed to be distracted. "I've got an idea," she said suddenly. "Why don't the three of us hit the ice cream parlor?" There were several outdoor places and shops geared toward confection and all the things that went with that. "My treat," she added, slanting a glance toward Chris and hoping to disarm any protests before they formed.

But Chris wasn't ready to take her up on her offer so quickly, even though he realized he'd been battling a rather intense attraction to her for the past forty-five minutes.

Or maybe because of it.

"We've inconvenienced you enough," he pointed out.

"Inconvenienced?" she echoed incredulously. "Seeing Joel is never an inconvenience," she told him, her eyes on the boy. "And when you add ice cream to that, well, there's just nothing better."

"You like ice cream?" Joel asked, surprised. Pleased.

"Like it?" she echoed. "Ice cream's my biggest weakness." Jewel grinned. "Never met a flavor I didn't like."

For his part, Joel looked as if he'd just fallen in love. "Really?"

Jewel traced an X over her breast and then held up her hand as if she were taking a solemn oath. "Absolutely."

It was only after the fact that she noticed that Chris was looking at the area where she'd traced the X. She felt herself growing warm despite the chill in the October air. Because of the medical complex's close proximity to the ocean, there was always a breeze.

"And after we get our cones, we can take a walk on the beach," she said. She was fairly certain that Joel hadn't done any of these aimless things, things that should have been part of a Southern California boy's life at this stage.

"Beach?" Chris questioned as if she had just said they were going somewhere halfway around the world.

Possibly there were two people who'd had deprived childhoods, she amended. "Yes, beach. You know, water, sand, the occasional seagull flying by making screeching noises."

He had things to do and research to catch up on. This would just be idling time away. Yet something kept him from saying that. Instead, he asked, "Aren't we keeping you from something?"

She took his tone to mean he was afraid she was on the clock. "I'm not charging you for this," she told him.

"That's not what I meant," he replied. Things were beginning to feel even more jumbled than they already were. Edges that had been so sharp before he'd found himself rushing to Blair Memorial were now dull and blurred. "It's just that we've taken up too much of your time."

Jewel looked at him for a long moment, wondering what kind of things were going on in his head. She hadn't said anything to indicate that she felt put out or taxed by any of this. She could only assume that he was using it as a cover.

"I'll let you know when it's too much," she promised

as they all climbed into the car. Jewel twisted around in her seat, looking at the boy sitting behind her. "Right now, I have this huge craving for an ice cream cone. How about you, Joel?" she wanted to know.

Joel pushed the metal tongue of his seat belt into the slot. "Yes, please," he replied.

That was all she wanted to hear. Jewel started up her vehicle. "Never could pass up sweet talk like that," she told her passengers with a grin.

To her surprise, Chris put his hand on the steering wheel, preventing her from pulling out of the parking space. She looked at the man quizzically, waiting.

"Only on one condition," he told her. His expression looked pretty somber.

"And that is?"

"I get to pay."

Her mouth curved then. She'd been prepared for something far more serious than a tug-of-war over the check.

"You're on," she answered.

"On what?" Joel wanted to know, confused.

On very shaky ground, apparently, Chris silently answered as the woman in the driver's seat said, "It's just an expression, honey. It means I'm taking him up on his suggestion."

"Oh."

Joel's curiosity might have been sated, but his was just taking hold, Chris thought as he stole another glance at the woman on his left. He had a feeling this was just the beginning.

The question remained—of what?

Chapter Seven

"None for me," Chris demurred when they walked into the small, old-fashioned ice cream parlor that backed up onto the beach.

Possibly because it was still early, the shop was only filled with sunshine. The six tables were all empty.

Taking out his wallet, Chris pulled out a twenty and, reaching around Jewel, he placed it on the stainless-steel counter just in front of her. "But you go ahead and order anything you want."

Jewel turned around to look at him. The whole point of coming here was to get ice cream cones. For *all* of them. "When was the last time you had an ice cream cone?"

He didn't see what that had to do with anything. "I can't remember."

Jewel frowned. "Now that's just plain wrong," she

told him. "I know you're not lactose intolerant because I saw you eat two slices of Theresa's cheesecake after the service." Theresa's cheesecakes were twice as rich as anything available on the open market. "If you can eat that, you can eat any dairy product." She turned back to the teenager behind the counter. "He'll have two scoops of rocky road, please."

In compliance, the teenager pushed two teeming scoops of rocky road onto a sugar cone. He carefully handed the creation to Jewel who in turn passed the cone on to Chris.

"Enjoy."

It wasn't a suggestion, it was a direct order.

Looking down at Joel, Jewel smiled encouragingly. "Okay, your turn. What'll you have?"

He thought for a moment. "Can I have two different kinds of scoops?"

"Absolutely," she guaranteed enthusiastically. "Even three different kinds of scoops if you want," she told him with a wink. "But you have to promise to eat *really* fast so the ice cream doesn't melt all over you."

"Two's enough," he answered her with the solemnity of a seasoned diplomat. "What's your favorite?"

She didn't hesitate. "Mint chocolate chip."

Joel said nothing, he just nodded. Standing up on his toes, he looked down into the various vats of ice cream. Confronted with over twenty flavors, Jewel assumed it was going to take the little boy some time to make up his mind. Instead, he made his choice quickly—one scoop each of mint chocolate chip and rocky road, a mixture of her choice and what she'd picked for Chris.

Jewel couldn't help wondering how much of that was because Joel liked the flavors and how much represented his desire to bond with both of them.

No doubt about it, he was a very complicated little boy.

"Okay, now what?" Chris asked once they each had their cones and he had collected his change.

Jewel thought she saw a hint of amusement in his eyes. Good, the man wasn't as wooden as he would have liked her to believe. "Now we eat our ice cream cones as we walk."

"At the same time?" Chris deadpanned, holding the door open for her and Joel.

Definitely amusement, she decided, walking out. "That's the general idea, but the ultimate choice is yours," she quipped. "Oh, and you might try enjoying yourself," she added.

"I don't need an ice cream cone to enjoy myself," he told her.

"No, but it doesn't hurt," she said, taking an appreciative lick of the top scoop on her own cone. Ordinarily, she didn't lick her ice cream, she took bites of it until it was gone. It disappeared faster that way, but she also got to enjoy it more quickly.

Jewel slanted a look at him as they proceeded down a short, sloped alleyway between two weathered bungalows, making their way to the beach just beyond. The sky, so bright and blue just a short while ago, was now overcast, hovering like a gauzy shroud over the horizon.

"I'll bite," she finally said. "What *do* you need to enjoy yourself?"

There was no hesitation. The world of science had been his haven for as long as he could remember. "Understanding a new concept that I never understood before."

It took her a second to make sense of what Chris was telling her. "You're talking about physics, aren't you?"

He nodded. "Science is very pure and its frontier is really endless. There's always something new to learn, to understand."

She could appreciate getting wrapped up in the pursuit of knowledge—but not to the exclusion of everything else.

"But while it might keep you up at night," she pointed out cheerfully, "it won't keep you warm."

He didn't see where she was going with this. "That was never a requirement."

She moved her shoulders in a vague shrug. "Maybe it should be," she countered. Before he could say anything in response, she turned her attention to Joel. They'd ignored the boy long enough, and while he didn't seem to mind, she minded *for* him. "Well, we're one step closer to getting you registered for school, Joel. Are you excited?"

He didn't answer. Instead, he emulated her earlier movement and made his thin shoulders rise and fall in a careless shrug.

"Maybe a little afraid?" she guessed. The look on his face as he raised his eyes to hers told Jewel she was closer to the truth than the little boy really wanted to admit.

He was deeper than children his age, she thought, but then, most children his age hadn't had to be a parent to one of their parents.

"It's okay to be afraid," she told him.

He stopped walking and looked up at her in surprise. "It is?"

"Uh-huh." She kept walking and Joel fell into step beside her on her right while Chris continued walking on her left. "As long as you don't let that fear make you hide from things," she qualified. "You've got to stand up to your fears and show them who's boss."

"What fears have you stood up to?" Chris asked, curious.

She hadn't expected him to interject a question. "Fear of failure."

She aroused his curiosity. People usually didn't. He found that interesting. "And have you? Failed?" he added.

"Nope, not yet," she answered brightly. Her shoe came in contact with something in the sand and she glanced down to see what it was. "Oh, look, Joel. A seashell." Jewel stooped to pick it up. It was small and, unlike so many other shells, it was in one piece, although heavily encrusted with sand. She blew on the shell to loosen some of the sand and then held it out to the boy. "If you hold it up to your ear, you can hear the ocean."

Instead of placing the shell to his ear to see if he could indeed hear the ocean, Joel turned and pointed toward the waves that were ebbing and flowing against the shore. "But the ocean is right there."

She pressed her lips together in order not to laugh. "When you take the seashell home," she told him, "you can still hear the ocean." There was a skeptical expression on the boy's face when he looked down at the shell. "I think," she said to Chris, lowering her voice as they resumed walking, "I have more to find than just Joel's father."

He wasn't following her. "Oh?"

"There's a missing childhood that needs to be restored," she told him, watching Joel as the boy walked a few steps ahead of them, at the moment engrossed in the way the waves were hugging the shore.

Chris didn't understand her concern. "There's nothing wrong with being serious."

"Once in a while, no," she agreed. "But all the time? He's five years old, Chris. At five, he shouldn't be analyzing statements for accuracy. He should be running around, playing games he made up and laughing."

Chris looked over toward his nephew. There were pictures of him in an old family album stored on his bookcase at home that could easily have been photographs of Joel. Moreover, he could relate to the way the boy behaved.

"My guess," he speculated, "is that he hasn't had a whole lot to laugh about."

Chris was probably right, she thought. "Well, then, he needs to be given something to laugh about." Jewel looked at him pointedly.

Oh, no. He was too busy to take on another responsibility. This was only temporary. "Talking to the wrong person," Chris replied. He finished the last of his cone. "He's just staying with me until you locate his father."

She suppressed the urge to tell him that Joel was his blood and that he should help him, not regard him as a hot potato to be passed to whomever was there to take him. Instead, she told him, "Time is relative. A lot can be accomplished in a short amount if you do it right." She wasn't making an impression, she thought. "Ever see *The Lost Weekend?* Ray Milland plays an alcoholic who got stone cold sober in a forty-eight-hour period."

Chris snorted. The actor's name was vaguely familiar only because his mother liked to watch old movies when he was a kid. "That's Hollywood back when things were oversimplified."

"True," she freely admitted, "but it's harder to kick a drinking habit than it is to laugh."

He supposed, in some twisted, convoluted way, that made sense. But he had a more basic question. "Do you get this involved in all your clients' lives?"

The answer to that was no. "Most of my clients are suspicious, sometimes vengeful people I wouldn't want to get involved with on a personal level," she told him. And then she smiled. "This is really a nice change from that." She'd felt herself becoming involved the moment she looked into Joel's sad brown eyes.

"So the answer's no?" he asked. He preferred things to be black and white.

"No, I don't usually get this involved," she confirmed,

then added, "I try very hard to keep my distance from people like that. Their lives are usually toxic."

"Then why do you do it?" he wanted to know. "You seem like a bright, intelligent person. There's got to be something else you could do for a living."

Probably, she acknowledged. But nothing that she would have wanted to do. She felt that investigation was her calling. Briefly, after graduating with a degree in criminology, she considered joining the police force. But she never liked taking orders.

"I'm good at this," she told him. "Good at getting to the bottom of things, at seeing what other people miss. At tracking down cheating spouses," she added with a sigh. Gathering evidence for divorces was, at the moment, her bread and butter. She could only hope that things would change soon. "It pays the bills, and every once in a while, I find a case that gets to me," she admitted. Jewel paused, looking at the boy. And then she turned her gaze pointedly to the man walking beside her. "If you ask me, I think you both need each other."

"What I need," he corrected, "is to get back to my work at the university. You can help me do that by finding his father."

It was what he had hired her to do. Who knew things would evolve to include another layer? Either way, it wasn't her place to force her sense of values on him.

"Right." Her cone finished, Jewel wadded up the napkin in her hand. "Speaking of which, I guess I'd better get back to that."

She was about to call out to Joel to tell him that

they were getting ready to leave, but Chris stopped her. "Wait."

Had she missed something? Jewel glanced around, but saw nothing that would make Chris want to pause. "For what?"

Instead of answering her, Chris took the napkin she'd just balled up from her hand. Opening it, he raised a section to her lips and gently wiped away the trace of green ice cream from the corner of her mouth.

As he eliminated the telltale drop, Jewel found herself holding her breath. Her eyes were on his. A warmth had slipped over her.

For a split second she'd thought...

But there was no reason to believe that anything out of the ordinary would happen. That was just her imagination running away with her.

She blamed it on the romantic comedy she'd watched on cable the night before.

"You had some ice cream there." Chris felt he needed to explain. He gave the napkin back to her.

She wasn't aware of taking it. "Thank you," she murmured.

The words, the moment, seemed to hang between them. It almost felt as if time had stood still for just a heartbeat.

Which was silly, because why should it? The man hadn't kissed her. He hadn't even touched her except through a napkin, for God's sake. Why did she suddenly feel like some virginal adolescent at the end of her very first date, waiting with baited breath for her first kiss?

She was light-years past that innocent, inexperienced girl. So why were her palms damp and her fingertips tingling?

Chris was still looking at her curiously, so she fumbled for words to explain. And because she was who she was, she told him the truth. And tried to make light of it.

"Funny, I thought you were going to kiss me."

She came so close to the truth, it caught him completely off guard. He had no idea that mind reading was part of her services.

"Why would I do that?"

She dismissed the idea with a shrug. "I don't know. Because you wanted to?" she guessed, still trying to keep the exchange light.

She didn't know the half of it, Chris thought. He wasn't sure why that was, either, but there was no denying—at least not to himself—that he had wanted very much to kiss her.

The feeling was as much a shock to him as it would have been to her had he said anything out loud. It had come over him out of the blue without any warning, like some rolling earthquake that left people shaken long after it was over. Shaken and doubting their own reactions.

"And if I had kissed you?" he pressed, wanting to hear her response.

What was he asking? Did he want to know if she would have protested? Not hardly. She was a flesh-and-blood woman, not some heroine in an eighteenth-century melodrama.

"That's easy," she told him. "I would have kissed you back."

He nodded, unaware that he was smiling. Broadly. "Good to know."

It left her wondering if he had just given her a glimpse of things to come.

"Joel," she called out to the boy. "We're going home."

"Whose?" he asked as he joined her.

Good question. "Yours." *At least it's yours for the time being.*

"Thanks for coming on such short notice," Chris repeated when she dropped them off at the house some twenty minutes later.

Being ready at a moment's notice was no big deal for her. Jewel considered it one of her assets. She laughed. "I'm a private investigator. The only kind of notice I get is short."

The sound of her laughter threaded through his system, putting him at ease. He realized that, without rhyme or reason, the sound created a feeling of well-being within him.

He forced himself to focus on her reply, not the effect she had on him. He still thought that hers was a strange choice of vocation for a woman. For so many reasons. "I never knew a woman who could get ready fast," he told her.

"How many women *have* you known?" She caught her lower lip between her teeth. *That was a really dumb thing to ask, Jewel,* she upbraided herself.

Rather than get annoyed—or give her an inflated

number—Chris resorted to an answer he thought she'd find acceptable, given her line of work.

"You're the private investigator," he told her. "You figure it out."

She paused, debating whether or not to give voice to her thoughts, or just to take the easy way out and say she'd get back to him on that. But it had been a rather strange morning. She decided she had nothing to lose by being honest with him.

"Your looks tell me that there should have been a lot of women in your life." She let him mull over the compliment for a moment before concluding, "But your dedication to your profession would seem to make that unlikely."

The latter was far closer to the truth than the former. "So which is it? A lot? Or none?" he asked.

"I'd split the difference." She glanced at her watch. How had it gotten to be so late? She'd only planned to give up an hour, not half the day. "I'm sorry, I've got to get going," she told him. Joel had stepped out of the vehicle and was now quietly standing beside his uncle, his beautiful brown eyes fixed on her. "I'll see you Monday, Joel," she promised. "You and I and your uncle have a date with Venado's school principal." She saw the concerned look create a small furrow between his eyes. The same one, it occurred to her, that Chris displayed when he was thinking. "Don't worry. That'll hurt even less than the shots."

Joel looked as if he doubted that, but he didn't contradict her out loud. "Can we go for another walk on the beach when we're finished?"

She knew that there were things she needed to do and that she could have easily turned the boy down. But she didn't want to. Just because she didn't want kids of her own didn't mean that she didn't like the species, she thought with a grin.

"Don't see why not." She looked over to her client. "Is that okay with you, Uncle Chris?"

He'd almost kissed her on the beach. Only enormous self-control and the need for self-preservation had saved him from that huge mistake.

But what about next time?

Next time was going to have to take care of itself. Chris nodded. "I suppose it can't do any harm."

Jewel flashed a grin. "It can only do some good. See you Monday, men," she said as she threw the car into Reverse and pulled out of the driveway.

She smiled.

It was going to happen. She was certain of it. One way or another, it was going to happen. Either while the case was still in progress, or afterward—she wasn't certain about the timing—but she knew it was going to be soon.

And hot. Very, very hot. He might be a man of few words but she had a feeling that he was a man of many moves.

She and Chris were going to make love. She could feel it in her bones and had never been so sure of anything in her life. Sure of that, and the fact that the person who had invented ice cream should be nominated for sainthood.

Chapter Eight

Always an early riser, Chris had already been up for almost three hours, and working for more than two of them, when he thought he heard the doorbell ring. Sitting on the sofa, deep in concentration, he looked up at the front door and frowned.

It was Sunday. It wasn't usual for people to just drop by unannounced during the week, much less on the weekend.

And then he remembered.

He *wasn't* home. He was in Rita's house. Maybe whoever was at the door had just come across one of the obituary notices that Jewel had sent out to the local newspapers and they were dropping by to see if it was true.

Well, he wasn't going to find out just sitting here, frowning, he told himself.

With a sigh, Chris put aside the scrap of paper he was currently making notes on.

First there was chaos, then there was order, he thought, looking around at the snowstorm of papers, envelopes and napkins he'd pressed into service, now scattered all over the coffee table. There were equations and/or notations on all of them. In their present state, he was the only one who could make any sense of what was there.

As he began to rise, Joel ran by him, heading toward the door. The boy looked almost eager.

"I'll get it," Chris called out to his nephew. He didn't want him getting into the habit of throwing open the door whenever someone knocked or rang the doorbell.

To his surprise, the boy didn't attempt to open the door. Instead, Joel scrambled up on the love seat that had its back against the window and peered out to see who was on their doorstep.

"It's Jewel!" Joel announced with the first bit of excitement he'd heard in the boy's voice.

"Jewel?" Chris echoed as he approached the front door.

What was she doing here? He didn't recall the private investigator saying anything about meeting with him today. Last he'd heard, she said she was coming along with them on Monday to get Joel registered for school.

Coming along.

The words mocked him. The woman wasn't "coming along," she was leading the way and he knew it. And he was damn grateful that she was. He hadn't a clue who to turn to for help when it came to doing all the ordinary things that having a five-year-old in your life entailed. He freely admitted that he would have been completely lost without her.

Opening the front door, Chris greeted her with "Were we supposed to get together today?"

"Hi, to you, too," she replied, amused.

Joel was right beside his uncle, shifting his weight from foot to foot, making no secret of the fact that he was happy to see her.

"Hi, Jewel!" he exclaimed even before she walked into the house.

Jewel grinned at the boy. "Now, that's a welcome," she pronounced. "Hi, yourself." She glanced up at Chris. "And to answer your question, no, we didn't make plans to get together today. But I like delivering my updates in person instead of over the phone." That wasn't entirely true, but he didn't have to know that. Let him think that she believed in the personal touch at all times. "Besides," she held up the two bags she'd brought with her, a warm, delicious aroma emanating from them, "I thought you might be running low on food, so I brought over breakfast. French toast, waffles, sausages *and* coffee," she recited.

She was about to place both bags on the coffee table, but she stopped before they made contact. The disarray registered. Her mother would have turned the mess into neat piles of paper in about five seconds. Ten tops.

"Making yourself at home I see," she commented. The next moment she was heading for the kitchen, which was still clutter-free, she noted.

"I was just working on something," Chris told her, following her into the next room.

"So I see," Jewel answered. She placed the bags on the kitchen table and turned toward him. "You want the food or the news first?"

Joel answered for both of them. "The food," he piped up.

"Food it is." That would have been her choice, too. Jewel's mouth curved as she raised her eyes to Chris's for a moment. He looked a little surprised. Obviously, the man wasn't accustomed to anyone making choices for him. "You've gotta be fast around a five-year-old—even a superintelligent one." Affection was spreading out long, slender fingers through her as she looked at Joel. The little boy in him was beginning to surface. There was hope.

"I'll keep that in mind," Chris murmured.

He opened first one cabinet, then another as he searched for plates. Rita's so-called system still hadn't quite sunk in yet, despite the number of days he'd already spent here. Cutlery took him a couple more moments to pinpoint as he opened several drawers before locating it. He finally placed plates and utensils on the counter in front of Jewel.

Though he'd made no comment on the choice she'd offered, Chris realized that he was in no hurry to hear the news Jewel was referring to. It wasn't that he'd settled in or gotten attached to the boy; it was just that if Jewel had managed to locate his ex-brother-in-law, it occurred to him that there would be no excuse to see her any longer. The thought of not seeing her anymore, he was surprised to realize, disturbed him.

Which disturbed him even further. Ordinarily, he didn't form attachments quickly.

So Chris did what he'd always accused the rest of the world of doing—he procrastinated. Until yesterday, he'd been eager to receive any news that would lead him to Ray. Now, he wasn't all that sure. There were mixed feelings swirling around in him.

The woman was fast, he noted. Just like that, the food Jewel had brought over was out of the bags and on the plates, waiting to be consumed.

With only minimal encouragement, Joel picked the French toast.

"These are good," Joel told her with wide-eyed wonder that she found both amusing and endearing.

"Glad you like them," she said. "French toast is my favorite breakfast, although I do like trying to fill up all the tiny spaces on a waffle. That way, when I eat the waffles, they're always extra sweet. How do you like yours? With syrup? Fruit?" she prompted when Joel didn't say anything.

Finally, he shrugged as he speared another piece of the French toast. "I don't know. I never had them before."

That was almost un-American, she thought, keeping the comment to herself. But if he'd never had waffles… "And the French toast?"

Joel shook his head, but he kept on eating. "No, never had that before, either."

She frowned. Some of her best childhood memories

had taken place around the breakfast table. "What did you have for breakfast?"

He shrugged again, quickly making short work of the pieces on his plate. "Anything I could find. Cereal sometimes," he added with an uncertain smile.

Something else they had in common, Chris thought. "I was a freshman in college before I realized that people ate anything besides cereal for breakfast," he told Joel.

The boy smiled and, just for a second, Chris felt as if he and Joel were sharing a moment. Something inside him stirred.

Meanwhile, Jewel was trying to relate and having a difficult time. Breakfast had always been there for her, as was love. She looked from the boy to his uncle. "You're kidding."

"Hardly ever" was Chris's deadpan response.

It took her a moment to realize that he was making a joke. Jewel laughed. "Sorry, forgot who I was talking to." Joel, she noticed, was already polishing off his portion. There wasn't even any syrup or powdered sugar left on the plate. "Can I interest someone in seconds?" she asked, looking pointedly at Joel.

The moment she asked, the little boy pushed forward his plate, a hopeful look in his eyes. He wasn't nearly as shy as he'd been when she first met him and that was a very good sign. She *knew* that there was a real boy under all that solemnity and knowledge. He just needed to be brought out.

"You got it," she told him. This time, she gave him a waffle instead of French toast.

Joel eyed the waffle for a moment, then hesitantly asked, "Can I have it your way?"

"Coming right up."

Very carefully, Jewel filled each and every square hole on the waffle's surface with maple syrup. There was just the right amount to accommodate one waffle. But that was enough.

Joel happily started to chew his way to satisfaction, beginning on one end and working his way to the other side.

"How about you?" Jewel turned toward Chris. "Can I interest you in seconds?"

What she could interest him in, Chris realized, his eyes covertly sweeping over the curves of her form, had nothing to do with food for the body. Sustenance for the soul was more like it.

Startled, his thoughts came to a skidding halt. Since when did he think like that? Was losing his sister and realizing that his only earthly ties now resided in a five-year-old boy—a five-year-old boy he was trying to hand over to someone else—responsible for throwing him off this way?

Or was it something else?

At thirty-two, most people didn't think about mortality, but he did.

Now.

Was it just the need to leave behind a footprint, however faint, to prove that he had passed through this life? He didn't think that way normally, but there was nothing really normal about the past week he'd been through.

She was waiting for him to answer. Chris could see it by the way she was looking at him. "No, thanks."

Jewel wasn't ready to give up just yet. "More coffee then?" she offered.

He could always drink more coffee. There were days when he started working at seven in the morning and didn't come home until after ten at night. Those were the days that he literally ran on coffee. It kept him going.

"Sounds good," he agreed.

She paused for a moment, studying him before going for the aforementioned coffee.

Something was quite obviously on her mind. It stirred his curiosity. "What?"

"Do you pay some kind of tariff if you use more than a few words in any given sentence?" she asked.

He'd never employed a plethora of words—unless it was on a paper he was writing. But then physics begged for the usage of more words to make concepts clear.

"Why use twelve words when you can get your meaning across with two?" he countered.

"Oh, I don't know." She sat down opposite him again, nursing her own cup of coffee. "Some people call it having a conversation. Adding a little bit of light and shading makes it more interesting for most people." *But, obviously, not for you.*

He looked at her over the rim of his cup. "You take care of that for both of us," he pointed out.

She didn't dispute that she'd never felt the need to be brief. "Granted, but it's nice to have someone else in the conversation."

There was amusement in his eyes as he promised, "I'll work on it."

She grinned at him. *Baby steps were still steps.* "That's all I ask."

Chris took in a deep breath. He supposed that there was no point in putting off the inevitable. He was going to find out sooner or later and he'd always believed in sooner rather than later. This had been a departure for him.

But now it was over. So, as he sipped his coffee, Chris braced himself for what she'd initially come to tell him. "You said that aside from wanting to bring over breakfast, you had some news."

She'd almost forgotten. There was something about being around this strong, silent man that turned her into someone with the mental acuity of a dandelion in the wind. "In a manner of speaking."

Out of the corner of her eye, she noticed that Joel had once again cleaned his plate and was now listening to her intently.

"In a manner of speaking," Chris repeated. "I don't follow."

"Well, I don't really know if you can call it news," she explained, "if you have nothing new to add."

Two and two came together very quickly. "Ray's old boss hasn't heard from him," he guessed.

It had taken her two hours of talking and following the man around his shop as he worked to get that non-information out of Bud Redkin. She nodded. "That about covers it."

"You think he's telling the truth?"

The question surprised her. Most people would have assumed that they were being told the truth. In her case, after the interview with Redkin, she'd checked the man out to see if he had any priors or if there had been any complaints lodged against him or his place of business. In both cases, the answer was no.

Which led her to her conclusion. "Yes, I think he was telling the truth. Redkin has nothing to gain by lying."

She was the expert, Chris thought. Part of him was disappointed with the outcome. The thing that gave him pause was that part of him *wasn't* disappointed. What was that about?

"So that's it?" he asked.

She couldn't gauge by his expression or tone if Chris was upset that she was unable to find Ray. But since Joel was within earshot, she refrained from asking. She didn't want the five-year-old coming away with the wrong impression. Genius or not, he still had feelings.

So she focused on business and reminded Chris what she'd said yesterday. "No, I still have other options to pursue."

She hadn't elaborated on that, he recalled. "Like what?"

She didn't like to talk about things until they were done, but she supposed that he did have the right to ask—and know. After all, he was paying for her services. "Like if Ray Johnson collected a paycheck any time since he left your sister, he might have filed a tax return." But she was taking nothing for granted. Even so-called law-abiding citizens sometimes "neglected" to file if they were getting paid off the books. And from what she'd gleaned from both Chris and Ray's old boss, Ray Johnson was not exactly a model citizen.

"What if he did?" Chris asked, for once taking a positive view. "The IRS isn't exactly known for their great penchant for sharing information."

Jewel took another sip of coffee and smiled over the rim. "There are ways" was all she said.

He found the mysterious smile on her face completely beguiling and stirring. He could feel its effects all the way down in his gut.

Maybe he was going off the deep end.

"What kind of ways?" he wanted to know, doing what he could to refocus his attention on why he'd hired her in the first place.

Jewel was shaking her head, her hair brushing along her shoulders. "Trust me," she counseled. "You're better off not knowing."

He interpreted her words the only way he could. "I don't want you getting caught doing something illegal on my account, Jewel."

"Don't worry." Instead of reassuring him that what she had in mind wasn't illegal, she just made him a promise. "I won't get caught."

She'd misunderstood, he thought. "No, I didn't mean—"

But Jewel started to laugh. "You have *got* to lighten up, Chris," she insisted, then smiled at him as she touched his shoulder. "Don't worry, this isn't anything that has a prison sentence attached to it." She still didn't want to get too specific. The less he knew, the less of a liability he was. "I'm just bending a few rules, not breaking any."

He didn't know if she was being honest with him, but he did know when to leave well enough alone. Not because he didn't want to be a co-conspirator or because he was such a straight arrow—there'd been a time when he wasn't. But if he knew what she was up to, he might feel obligated to stop her, and he had a feeling that Jewel Parnell was not a woman who was easily stopped. He'd rather not have that confrontation if he could possibly avoid it.

Jewel supposed he deserved a crumb more than he was getting. So she offered it to him. "I know a guy who owes me a favor and he knows a guy... Let's just leave it at that."

But she had raised another question in his mind, a question he wouldn't have normally wondered about. But for some reason he did when it came to Jewel.

"What kind of a favor?" he asked her.

She gave him just the bare bones. She had never been one to brag. "His sister was kidnapped in lieu of payment for some drugs. I made things happen to get her back."

Chris looked at her for a long, pregnant moment. Maybe he didn't socialize all that much, but he knew that most people would have turned that into a half an hour story, emphasizing their part in it and magnifying all their deeds. But Jewel just seemed to shrug it off.

Was that modesty?

Or was it something else?

"Now who's economizing on words?" Chris asked her.

Jewel responded with a grin. "Maybe your influence is rubbing off on me," she told him.

When she turned to say something to Joel since she'd left the boy out of the conversation, she suddenly realized that he was no longer in the room. That was really odd, she thought. She hadn't heard him leave.

And why *would* he leave? Every other time she'd interacted with Chris, Joel had stayed close by.

"Where's Joel?" she asked Chris. Maybe he had noticed the boy wandering off.

Anything Chris might have said in response to the question was drowned out by the sudden, heart-wrenching wail they heard coming from the rear of the house.

Jewel was on her feet instantly.

The cry had come from Joel.

Chapter Nine

With Joel's distraught cry ringing in his ears, Chris rushed to his nephew's room, getting there just ahead of Jewel.

At the very least, he expected to find Joel lying on the floor, hurt and bleeding, a victim of some kind of bizarre accident. But, at first glance, there didn't seem to be anything out of order in the room. No books on the ground, covering him, no chair that had toppled backward with Joel as its occupant.

Instead, his nephew was standing in front of his small, secondhand bookcase, sobbing as if he were never going to be able to stop.

Though Chris was the first one to run into the room, it was Jewel who was the first to get to the boy. Dropping to her knees, she quickly looked him over to find the cause for this heartbreaking display of grief. Not finding any obvious injuries, she put her hands on Joel's heaving shoulders and asked, "Honey, what's wrong? What is it? Please tell me."

Joel couldn't answer her at first. The sobs were all but choking him. He was crying as if his heart had been shattered into a million tiny pieces.

Her hands still on his shoulders, Jewel quickly scanned the room, looking for clues. It crossed her mind that Joel might be having a delayed reaction to his mother's death. But what had triggered it?

"Is it about your mother, Joel?" Her voice was kind, coaxing.

Still trying to catch his breath, the boy could only point to the bookcase.

Jewel felt helpless and frustrated. Had Joel seen a photograph or something else that he associated exclusively with his mother? Was that what had brought on this uncontrollable flood of tears?

"What is it, honey? I don't see—"

And then, the second she said it, she did. She saw what had reduced the little boy to tears. Saw what had served as a catalyst.

In the middle of the books, knickknacks and things that only a little boy's imagination could turn into treasures, she saw a dingy-looking fishbowl. There was a crack on the side of the glass, near the top. But that had no bearing on its function as a home for the bowl's occupant. Or, more accurately, former occupant. For the turtle who had obviously been living there appeared to be dead.

There was no movement, no struggling on the turtle's part. He was on his back, and his tiny feet were still.

Very gingerly, aware that Chris was watching her every move, Jewel reached into the bowl and extracted the turtle. She brushed a fingertip across his head, but there was no reaction. No attempt to bite her or to even pull his head into his shell. She had no idea what a turtle was supposed to feel like, but the one in her hand was room temperature. And very, very dead.

She laid him back down and turned to Joel. "I'm sorry, Joel. He's gone."

"He was my friend," the boy said in between hiccupping sobs.

Watching this, Chris was utterly stunned. "You're crying over a *turtle?*" he asked incredulously. "Seriously?"

Jewel could see what was coming. Making a quick decision, she said, "Excuse us for a second, Joel. I have to talk to your uncle."

With that, she took hold of Chris's arm and firmly pulled him into the hall. She could feel him staring at her in surprise, but she didn't want to take a chance on further hurting Joel's feelings. She understood what was going on, even if Joel didn't, and she needed to explain it to Chris. Things were *not* what they seemed.

"He didn't blink during the funeral," Chris said. "His *mother's* funeral. There wasn't a single tear before, during or after. Not one tear," he emphasized, holding up his finger. "And now, just because that stupid reptile croaks, Joel's crying as if his whole world is caving in on him."

He couldn't understand. Maybe Rita hadn't been the world's greatest mother. Maybe her name wasn't even in the top-qualifying one million. But how could Joel be crying for a turtle when he hadn't cried for his own mother?

"It *is* caving in on him," she assured Chris. "Now, be quiet and stop talking."

His eyes widened in disbelief. She was telling *him* to be quiet? Had the whole world just gone crazy?

"It's displacement," she informed him, her voice steely even though she was whispering. "Joel didn't cry after his mother died because being in restrained control of his emotions was the way he'd been taught to behave all his life. He has been the man of the house for as long as he could remember. He didn't have time for tears, for feeling sorry for himself. He had to take care of his mother.

"And when his mother died, he behaved as stoically as he always had, internalizing his grief. But the turtle was his pet. When he was playing with the turtle, he was just a normal little boy. A normal little boy with vulnerable feelings. When he walked into the room and found the turtle dead, that brave little soldier he was projecting just crumbled. Don't let this scene fool you. Joel's not just crying over losing his turtle, he's crying over everything. But predominantly, he's crying over losing his mother."

Chris considered what Jewel had just said. He supposed it was plausible. It wasn't as if he'd never heard of displacement. He just didn't associate that kind of multilayered response with a five-year-old.

"This PI license you have," he asked, a touch of sarcasm hiding his concern, "does it come with a degree in psychology?"

Jewel smiled at him. He understood. "I minored in it," she told him. She didn't know if he realized that she was serious. "But it doesn't take a degree to connect the dots." Belatedly, she realized that she was still holding on to Chris's arm. With a twinge of self-consciousness, she released it, then turned around and walked back into Joel's room.

"Joel, would you like to have a funeral service for—" It suddenly occurred to Jewel that she didn't know what to call the expired turtle. "I'm sorry, what was your turtle's name?"

Joel wiped the dampness from his cheeks with the back of his wrist. "Mr. Turtle."

"Very neat and succinct," she said with an approving nod. "Would you like to have a funeral service for Mr. Turtle?"

His eyes darted toward the fishbowl, then back up at her. "Can I do that?"

She draped her arm around Joel's shoulders. "Of course you can. We can put Mr. Turtle in a shoe box—or wrap him up in a handkerchief the way they used to do in biblical times," she amended when she saw the disheartened look in the boy's eyes at the mention of a shoe box. Apparently, there weren't any to be had. One glance at the worn sneakers he was wearing told her that shoes hadn't been a priority for his late mother.

"They wrapped up people in handkerchiefs?" Joel asked, confused.

"They called them shrouds. They were big, white cloths, but for the sake of argument, you could say that they were made out of the same kind of material that handkerchiefs are these days." She looked over his head toward Chris. "I'm sure your uncle can donate a handkerchief to the cause so that we can bury Mr. Turtle in the backyard."

The idea of a funeral for a turtle had sounded rather absurd to him, but Chris told himself he wasn't going to say anything. Until she mentioned the word *bury*. Leaning into her, Chris whispered, "Do you have any idea how hard the soil is around here? It's like trying to dig into clay. Not exactly easy."

She wasn't about to be put off. Joel needed this kind of closure. Needed to feel as if he were in control of something.

"But you have muscles," she told Chris with a smile. She patted one of his biceps to reinforce her statement. "You'll manage."

Joel dried off the last of his tears, wiping away a trail that had made it all the way down to his chin, and ventured an almost hopeful smile in Jewel's direction. "Can we do it now?"

"Absolutely. All we need is a handkerchief and a shovel." She turned toward Chris, intending to collect the former. "Can you help us out here, Uncle Chris?"

Chris suppressed a sigh. He still thought that this was going a bit far, but if it helped the boy deal with his grief, displaced or not, he supposed he could go along with it.

Handing over his handkerchief, he said, "I'll go see if there's a shovel in the garage," and walked out of his nephew's bedroom.

In the end, Jewel prevailed upon Chris to go to the hardware store to buy a shovel. There wasn't one in the garage, and digging in the claylike soil with a spoon— the only thing in the house that came close to any kind of digging implement—would take much too long.

An hour later, armed with a shovel and a handkerchief, preparations for the funeral service got underway. Chris dug a small hole, swallowing a few choice words as he went about the chore.

For Joel's sake, Jewel saw to it that the ensuing service was conducted with all the solemnity of a real funeral. That included having a few well-chosen words said over the tiny, handkerchief-wrapped form that was now lying in repose in the shallow hole in the backyard.

She had Joel go first, and then she followed, giving the deceased pet his proper due as best she could. "We won't think of this as an end, Mr. Turtle, because it isn't. It's just the beginning. The beginning of a brand-new adventure. You've gone on to a place where there's always enough to eat and everyone gets along with everyone else. Rest well, Mr. Turtle. You've earned it."

She saw Joel gratefully smiling at her and she knew she'd struck the right notes.

Concluding her eulogy, she turned to Chris. When he made no move to say anything, she coaxed, "Your turn."

Chris scowled, confused. He was sure he'd heard wrong. "My what?"

"Your turn," she repeated. When there still was no response, she fed him the rest of the line. "To say a few words over Mr. Turtle," she prodded.

The look in Chris's eyes said she had to be kidding. That hope died the next moment as she continued to look straight at him, waiting.

The woman had a stubborn streak a mile wide, he thought. Stepping forward the way she and Joel had done, Chris kept his head bent, not out of any need to show respect for the dead turtle, but because if he looked up, he was certain his impatience at having to go through with this charade, for a *turtle* for God's sake, would be evident.

"I never got to know you, Mr. Turtle, but I'm sure you were a very good pet for Joel. Now you're in heaven. I guess you don't have to worry about anyone beating you in any races anymore. Enjoy yourself."

Jewel pressed her lips together to keep from laughing. Chris looked like the epitome of discomfort. He needed to be let off the hook. "That was very nice, Chris," she said softly. Turning to the boy, she asked, "Joel, would you like to throw some dirt on the shroud?"

"Like we did with Mama?" he asked.

She nodded. "Just like that," she assured him. She was rewarded with a look of pure contentment on Joel's face.

Bending down, he took a handful of dirt and threw it into the small grave. Jewel followed suit, making certain that she distributed the dirt evenly. Then she looked at Chris.

To her relief, he didn't roll his eyes the way she had expected him to. Instead, he just bent down, took a handful of dirt and threw it on top of the handkerchief-wrapped turtle.

"I'll finish up," he volunteered.

She had been prepared to do it herself and smiled with no small relief when he made the offer. "That would be very nice of you, Chris."

Another voice joined hers. "Thank you, Uncle Chris," Joel said.

Chris caught himself thinking that the look on the boy's face made the whole charade more than worth it. Maybe Jewel did know what she was doing, he thought, as he slowly drizzled a shovel full of dirt over the tiny grave he'd just dug.

The satisfied feeling and warmth that ensued was a very nice dividend. Without realizing it, he slanted a glance at Jewel, because she was the heart of it all. Shining a light so that he could follow.

Jewel stayed with them another hour or so, but then she said that she had somewhere to be. Joel took the information in stride because he was five, but Chris had no such luxury to fall back on. He wondered what it was that she had to do and where she was going.

He came close to asking, but he didn't. Instead, he walked her to her car in the driveway.

"Thanks for being my interpreter," he said to her once

they were outside. When she raised a quizzical eyebrow, he explained, "I don't speak 'kid' very well."

The admission made her grin. "You were one, once," she reminded him.

"I'll take your word for it," he answered. "My memory doesn't go back that far."

She wouldn't accept the excuse. "Sure it does. Just open yourself up and you'll remember," she promised. He obviously needed a little more convincing and prodding, she thought. "You were his age once, and I think the two of you have more in common than you realize."

He supposed that she might have a point. There were things that Joel said or did that stirred vague memories for him, memories that insisted on remaining teasingly just out of reach.

And then Jewel smiled at him. Really smiled. It was that smile that seemed to have generous helpings of sunshine in it. Just seeing it made him want to bask within its rays.

"You know, all disclaimers aside, for a novice, you did pretty well today," she told him.

He shrugged. The credit didn't belong to him. The sun was out now, having burned away the last layers of overhanging fog. A few stray rays were weaving themselves into her hair, giving it golden highlights. He caught himself wanting to thread his fingers through it to see if those strands felt any different from the rest.

"Only because I was following your lead," he finally managed to say, forcing himself to focus on the conversation. He didn't want her to go just yet. "You sure you don't have any kids?"

"Absolutely positive," she assured him. "It would be something I'd know. As for relating to kids, it comes easy to me. Maybe it's because I never grew up myself," she added tongue in cheek.

His eyes traveled the length of her form, a form that by any definition was nothing short of mouth-wateringly gorgeous. "Oh, you grew up, all right," he told her. "Trust me."

Chris's tone, unintentionally warm and sexy, sent another wave of heat zigzagging its way up and down her spine, rendering her momentarily speechless. It took her a minute to regain the use of her tongue.

"Was that a compliment?"

A compliment, not about the quality of her work, but about her body, sounded much too personal. The situation called for maintaining a professional distance between them, at least until he was no longer retaining her services.

"An observation," he countered.

"I see." He might be fooling himself, she thought, but he wasn't fooling her. She smiled indulgently. "Thank you for your 'observation.'"

He stared off over her head, his face expressionless. "You're welcome."

"What time do you want me over here tomorrow to help get Joel registered for school?" she asked.

The whole time, he thought.

That was when he realized that he really didn't want her to leave. She made dealing with Joel easier. With her here, he felt less out of his element, less like a fish out of water. It was better for the boy, too. And if he found her presence more than just passably pleasant, well, that was an added bonus.

The fact that this wasn't "business as usual" for him was something he wasn't entirely willing to explore right now. But perhaps his sister's untimely death had made him acutely aware that there wasn't an infinite allotment of time available. Perhaps there was more to life than just solving the perfect quadratic equation.

But he knew that saying any of this would give Jewel the wrong impression—or maybe the right one; he didn't know. In any case, he couldn't afford to have her know how attracted he was to her. Since he was paying her for her services some sort of conflict of interest would definitely arise if he wound up sleeping with her, as well.

Right now, he needed to keep things simple. And, most importantly, he needed to have her find Ray. He was fairly certain that she was good at her job. Once his life was his own again, maybe then he would be free to follow up on these feelings he was having.

So he pretended to think about her question, then asked, "How does ten o'clock sound?"

She had always been, almost against her will, an early riser, a habit she'd picked up from her mother. "I can come over earlier," she volunteered. "That way, you can get this registration over with and maybe get a chance to put in some time at the university the rest of the day." She knew he hadn't been there in a week, ever since he'd found out about his sister's death.

The thought of touching base with the university, of

perhaps going in and teaching one of his classes, was exceedingly tempting to him. Being a professor had always been his goal. It was what he did, what he was. But everything was up in the air right now.

Besides, what would he do with his nephew? He couldn't just conveniently stick him out of the way in a filing cabinet.

He was surprised that Jewel hadn't thought of that. "As much as I'd like to, I can't bring Joel with me to sit in on my classes, and I can't just leave him at home."

"I know. Monday my mother goes over her books, and then she and her friends have this poker game they play once a week. I think I can persuade her to alter her plans a bit to include Joel. He'll have three grandmothers-in-training fussing over him. How great is that?"

He should have known she would have thought this through. "Sounds good," he agreed. "You have an answer for everything, don't you?"

She looked at him. There was an ache inside her, an ache that felt as if it were growing larger every time she was alone with him. Logic dictated that she not act on impulse, but emotions told her the exact opposite, leaving her stuck in the middle, undecided and torn.

She knew there was no such thing as "happily ever after"; she'd had proof of that over and over again. But she also knew that there was the "enjoyable now." And now was all there was.

What would you do if I kissed you, Chris? Would you back away, saying there were lines not to be crossed, or would you kiss me back?

"No, not everything," she answered quietly, addressing his comment.

There was something about the expression on her face and the tone of her voice that spoke to him. Or, more accurately, that got to him.

And maybe that was why it happened, although he really wasn't sure. His reasoning process became a blur.

All Chris knew was that one moment, he was talking to her, the next, Jewel was in his arms and he was kissing her.

The way he really wanted to.

Chapter Ten

Jewel was aware of everything. Of the look in his eyes, of her heart as it pounded. Of his mouth as it came closer to hers.

It was as if it were all happening in slow motion.

She was afraid that if she moved, if she so much as breathed, the spell would be broken and she'd be snapped out of this temporary, delicious fantasy that had somehow overtaken her.

But the moment his lips touched hers, she knew that this wasn't a fantasy.

It was real.

Very, very real.

Real enough to up her body temperature by at least several degrees. The last time she felt this hot, she'd had a raging fever.

Savoring the moment, the intoxicating excitement,

she wrapped her arms around Chris's neck, gave herself up to the feeling and kissed him back.

He should be apologizing for taking liberties. And he would. In a minute. But Chris wanted to enjoy the moment, the overpowering sensation just a little longer. He was aware of his arms tightening around her, aware of the delicious taste of her lips permeating his consciousness. Jewel tasted of all things sweet and tempting.

A fire surged through his veins.

God, was he losing his mind?

Or finding it?

With effort, Chris made himself pull back—before he made another move forward that he was going to regret. Because he wanted to make love with her. And that was completely crazy, not to mention out of the question.

Avoiding her eyes for a moment, Chris coughed, clearing his throat. Buying some time.

"I'm sorry," he finally said, raising his eyes to hers. "I don't know what came over me. I don't have anything to say in my defense except that I haven't been myself lately."

It took her a moment to pull herself together and another to catch her breath. She could still feel her pulse racing. She was far from a novice at this, but no one had ever made her lose her train of thought before just by kissing her. It usually took a lot more "undercover" activity than what had just transpired to make her forget her name, rank and serial number.

There was no denying that Chris was sexy. He had already gotten her blood going with just a look or a word, but she definitely hadn't been prepared for this. Talk about still waters running deep. This was like falling through a crack in the earth and encountering a subterranean wild river.

"Well, tell whoever was just substituting for you that's it's okay." *And make him come by again.* "I'm not about to go all 'indignant feminist' on you." She took a breath as subtly as possible. Her pulse was still sending out scrambled Morse code. "We're both consenting adults here." Searching for words in the jumble that now comprised her brain, she ran her tongue along her lips and tasted him again. Her stomach tightened in futile anticipation. "Very adult," she added under her breath.

He scrutinized her, as if uncertain whether or not to take her at her word. "So then you're not offended or angry?"

She grinned. Hadn't he gleaned that from the way she'd kissed back? "So far from angry that we're not even on the same continent."

"And you'll still come tomorrow?" he wanted to know, then quickly added, "For Joel?"

Even if I had to walk barefoot in the snow. "Count on it." She couldn't have pulled off a deadpan expression right now if her very life depended on it. The grin on her lips came from deep within her and it was far too difficult to suppress. The best she could do was repeat the words he'd just said. "For Joel."

He held the door open for her as she slid behind the wheel. "Thank you," he said.

No, thank you, she thought. Not trusting her voice, she merely nodded as she started up the car and put it into Reverse.

Jewel had barely gotten back onto the road before her cell phone began to ring. Was it Chris? Had he decided to ask her to come back, using some flimsy excuse to make her return? She would have accepted anything, it didn't matter. But because of their situation, the ball was in his court and the play was his to make.

One eye out on the road, she fumbled in her glove compartment for her Bluetooth headset, something she hated dealing with but it was either that or pull off the road in order to answer her phone. There was a third alternative, but even if she wasn't hoping that the call was coming from Chris, she wasn't the type to let her calls go to voice mail unless she just couldn't get to her phone in time.

The cell was about to ring for the fourth time—at which point it *would* go to voice mail—when she finally pushed the silver button on her headset that allowed her to answer the phone.

She realized that she was nervous as she said, "Parnell Investigations."

"About time you answered. So, do you have anything 'new' to tell me?"

Daydreams unceremoniously bit the dust. It wasn't Chris on the other end of the call; it was her mother. Acting as if she knew what had just happened between her and Chris.

How in God's name had her mother known that Chris had just kissed her?

Calm down, Jewel. She's not a seer, she doesn't know. She's just being Mom and checking up on you, the way she always does.

"Nothing new," Jewel said innocently. The light turned yellow and for once, she slowed down instead of flying through it. Talking to her mother always took the edge off her reflexes. It would be just her luck to have a car run a red light and come plowing into her. Better slow than sorry. "I'm still looking for Joel's father."

"And you're hoping to find him in Joel's house?" There was a touch of mocking in her mother's voice. "Do you think he might be hiding in the closet? Or possibly inside Chris's mouth? I assume that was why you'd locked lips with him, hoping to suck out Joel's father."

"How did you—? Okay, this is getting positively creepy now, Mom. How the hell did you know that he kissed me?"

"Don't swear, Jewel," Cecilia admonished. "I taught you better than that. As for how, you're not the only Parnell who's capable of finding things out, dear."

"You're not a Parnell, Mom," Jewel pointed out, a fact that her mother had repeated to her more than once. "At bottom, you're an O'Hara."

Cecilia snorted. "I put up with your father's mother for ten years before the old crone died. I earned that name."

Jewel remembered how trying and demanding her father's mother had been. There were several times when she'd been surprised that her mother hadn't just lost it and strangled the woman. Anyone familiar with Fiona Parnell wouldn't have ever blamed her.

"No argument here."

She heard her mother chuckle. "Well, now, that's a novelty."

Oh, no, she wasn't going to get sucked down this path again. "Are you going to tell me how you knew that Chris kissed me or are you going to continue to regale me with your snappy patter?" And then, before her mother could say anything to enlighten her, the explanation suddenly came to Jewel. She'd heard a car go by when Chris was kissing her. "You drove by, didn't you?"

Now that she thought about it, the vehicle had sounded like it was slowing down, but she'd just thought that it was a nosy person wanting to watch them kiss.

She'd been right. It *was* a nosy person. It was her mother. She should have known.

"That was you in the car, wasn't it, Mother?"

"I don't know what you're talking about."

She could almost see her mother tossing her head, her still beautiful hair flying over her shoulder. The woman could have been an actress.

"I'm talking about hearing a car slow down, then pick up speed and drive away. That was you. Don't bother to deny it." She shook her head. "Mother, what possible reason could you have had to drive by his house like some deranged stalker? They have laws against stalking in this state," she warned. "You could be arrested."

"Don't get so dramatic, Jewel. I wasn't stalking," Cecilia protested with a touch of indignation. "I was just going to stop by to see how they were doing. I had a batch of Theresa's chocolate chip cookies with me— she's experimenting again," she said by way of an aside. "But I got my answer at least as to how Chris was doing without having to stop the car."

Jewel braced herself. She could hear her mother's grin over the phone and she knew what was coming.

"So, I did good, didn't I, Jewel?"

She'd guessed right, Jewel thought. "Mom, if by that you mean that you were right to refer his case to me because you thought that I could find his missing ex-brother-in-law, then yes, you 'did good.'"

"You know perfectly well that's not what I mean, Jewel." There was more than a trace of impatience in her mother's voice.

"Maybe," she allowed. "But I'm not going to dignify what you're alluding to with an answer. Look, Mom, I'm on the road—"

"You have that thing, that greentooth—"

"Bluetooth, Mother," she corrected not for the first time. "It's called a Bluetooth."

"Whatever," Cecilia dismissed. "You've got that thing to talk into so the police can't give you a ticket." She got back to what she'd wanted to say. "Why do you have to be so stubborn about everything?"

"It's in my genes," Jewel answered matter-of-factly. "I get it from my mother."

"You like him, Jewel," Cecilia insisted. "I've watched you. At the cemetery, at the house. I can see that you like him."

Her mother was adopting far too simplistic a view of things. It didn't matter if she liked him or not. She wasn't about to get involved in the manner her mother was hoping that she would. "That has nothing to do with anything."

"Yes, it does." Her mother's tone said she knew better.

"If I wasn't the one who'd sent him your way, you'd probably be wondering if he was 'the one' by now. But because I arranged this, because *I* like him, you're digging in your heels and resisting getting involved with him."

Jewel didn't have time to argue. Besides, there was no winning when it came to her mother. "I *am* involved with him, Mom. I'm handling his case."

Her mother laughed shortly. "You should be handling something else."

"Mom!" Jewel almost swerved into the next lane. Fortunately, there was no car in that space. Recovering, she blew out a breath. She and her mother had an open relationship, but her mother had never been this bluntly direct before.

"You're not fourteen anymore—and even at fourteen, you were more knowledgeable than I was comfortable about. My point is that life is pretty short and if a decent, intelligent man crosses your path, you shouldn't immediately run the other way just because he has your mother's blessings. And if that man happens to be a hottie, well that's all the better."

Her mother was obviously going through her second childhood, Jewel decided. "I'm not comfortable with your calling a guy a hottie, Mom. What's come over you, anyway?"

"I'm worried about you," Cecilia said.

"Then stop worrying," Jewel told her. "There's nothing to worry about, anyway."

"If you were a mother, you'd understand. Mothers worry. It's what we do. And we don't stop until we're dead because there's always something to worry about. The fact remains that Christopher Culhane is very much a 'hottie' and if you pretend that you're not interested, some other woman's going to come by and snatch him up," Cecilia predicted.

"And then she can go through the divorce instead of me," Jewel concluded. This time, she pressed down on the accelerator, flying through the yellow light before it turned red.

"You're not even married yet, Jewel. Why would you even be *thinking* about getting a divorce?"

Her mother lived in a very sheltered world, despite everything she'd been through. She'd married her very first boyfriend. She and her two best friends remained married to the same men until the disclaimer, "til death do us part," became a reality. All three women had had good marriages. The world that existed these days was completely foreign to her mother and her friends.

"Because, sadly, it happens, Mom. It happens a lot." She thought of all the cases she'd handled since she began her career five years ago. Every one of the cheating spouse cases had ended in divorce. Those were devastating odds. "Do you think that most of my clients got married thinking they were going to be divorced within five, ten, fifteen years?"

She heard her mother sigh. "I can't speak for anyone else, Jewel."

"Sure you can, Mom." She almost missed her turn and made a sharp right at the last minute. The driver behind her blasted his horn. "You're trying to speak for me."

"That's different. I'm your mother. Everything you do

is my business, whether you know it or not. Whether you like it or not," Cecilia added with emphasis. "Because if you're not happy, I'm not happy."

"I'm happy, Mom, I'm happy," Jewel said through clenched teeth.

"No one's happy alone, Jewel," her mother stubbornly insisted.

She had her there, Jewel thought. "I'm not alone, Mom. I have you. And my friends."

"That is not the same thing, Jewel, and you know it. I'm talking about someone to share your life with—and that doesn't mean a dog, either," Cecilia interjected quickly, anticipating her daughter's next words.

This was going to go on indefinitely unless Jewel took some drastic measures.

"What, Mom? What did you say? Sorry, Mom, I seem to be losing you. I'm going through an underpass." To underscore that, Jewel cupped her hand around the headset and made some garbled, swishing noises, doing her best to imitate static.

"I'll talk to you later," Cecilia said, raising her voice to be heard above the so-called static. With a sigh, she hung up the phone.

Jewel followed suit, shaking her head. Only her mother could make a promise sound like a threat, she thought. And this was only the beginning. She knew her mother wasn't about to back off. Not now that both her friends had finally been successful in their matchmaking efforts. They'd brought their daughters together with men they'd met through their chosen careers—even Jewel had to admit they were practically perfect for her friends in every way. So her mother was not about to just give up because she'd asked her to.

If anything, that was like waving a red flag in front of a bull. Her resistance just gave her mother more of an incentive to keep pushing. And no one under the sun could push like her mother could. Not even Maizie. Her mother could keep this up indefinitely.

She didn't have to ask to know that this—not running a house-cleaning service—was what her mother felt was her calling, her destiny. Her mother was going to get her married or die trying.

"I appreciate the effort, Mom," Jewel said out loud to her absent mother as she made her way up a freeway ramp, "but there are no guys out there who won't break your heart without a backward glance. All the good ones are spoken for or dead."

While she fervently prayed that Nikki and Kate had lucked out and gotten two very rare men who meant what they said about loving them until the day they died, she truly doubted that lightning would strike a third time in a given space.

These days, if you knew three couples, chances were better than even that two of those couples were on their way to getting a divorce for one reason or another. And if they weren't now, they would be soon. She should know. She'd handled the back end of too many cases, gathering proof for a spouse who was either vengeful, grieving or, on rare occasions, in denial, and she'd hoped that she could somehow prove that they had a right to be optimistic.

Those were always the toughest cases for her because,

once she'd collected evidence to the contrary, she knew her news would not be well received. Once or twice she'd actually thought of lying, of burying the information and telling the client that her husband really was working late rather than seeing a younger woman.

But she had an obligation to her clients to do the best job she could, even if it ultimately meant that her report would be greeted with tears or rants.

What all these broken marriages and broken promises had taught her was that it was better just to enjoy the moment, to enjoy the temporary thrill. *Forever* was a word for storybooks. Realistically, it had nothing to do with the vows exchanged in a marriage. She had made her peace with that, which was why she wasn't even looking for the "perfect mate."

However, if she were looking for the perfect specimen of the male gender, she doubted that she could come up with anything better than Professor Christopher Culhane. On that score, her mother was right. She certainly wouldn't kick the man out of bed if the occasion arose.

She smiled to herself, thinking of her mother's response to that. More than likely, her mother would see it as the beginning of something lasting.

"Sorry, Mom," she said as she wove her way around a slow-moving SUV. "That's the best I can do."

The "best" seemed pretty good to her from where she sat, Jewel mused. The more she thought about it, the better it sounded to her. The very thought of winding up in bed with Chris, of making love with him, got her blood moving *very quickly* through her veins.

If the man made love the way he kissed, she might just have to invest in fireproof sheets if they wound up coming together at her place.

Her mouth curved as she thought about that. It was definitely something to consider.

Jewel shook herself free of the fantasy that was taking hold. Right now, she had to follow up a hunch she'd had earlier. She didn't want Chris to think that he was wasting his money by hiring her.

With effort, Jewel focused her mind on the case and not on the man who was asking her to find Ray Johnson. It wasn't easy, but after a while, she managed.

Chapter Eleven

Like an evening shadow slipping across a room, it slowly dawned on Chris that he was looking forward to seeing Jewel.

He told himself that it was only because she was so good with his nephew, understanding the boy in ways he couldn't even begin to fathom. And it was because of that, not any deeper, more personal reason, that he kept glancing at his watch every few minutes. When he wasn't looking at his watch, he was looking out the window, anticipating the moment that she'd pull into his driveway and stride up the front walk.

Somehow, he couldn't quite snow himself.

For the most part, Chris felt he was keeping his thoughts pretty much under wraps—until Joel's voice penetrated his thoughts. "Do you think that she won't come?"

"What?" Preoccupied, Chris only heard the question after several seconds had gone by. It was as if there were a five-second time delay going on in his brain.

Patiently—with far more patience than he felt—Joel explained, "Jewel said she'd be here."

Chris didn't know if Joel was distressed, or if he was trying to reassure himself—or Chris. In any case, Chris felt compelled to take on the role of the calm adult, even though he was hardly feeling calm.

"If Jewel said she'll be here, she'll be here." He glanced again toward the window, from this angle seeing only the withering olive tree directly in the front yard. "She's probably just stuck in traffic."

Joel took this as a plausible excuse, nodding his head. "It'd be easier if she stayed here."

"This isn't her home," he explained to the boy.

Joel looked at him as if the answer he'd just tendered didn't really make sense. "It's not yours, either, but you're here 'cause it's easier."

Chris laughed, shaking his head. He'd love to see this kid in high school on the debating team. "How old are you really?"

Joel's small eyebrows narrowed, scrunching together over the bridge of his nose. "Five."

Chris wasn't given to touching, to drawing in close, but something kept cutting through his reserve. He ruffled Joel's hair. "You're very bright, you know that, right?"

Joel nodded. When he responded, he sounded like a learned old soul. "Yeah, I know that."

It was at that moment that it occurred to Chris that

perhaps placing Joel in kindergarten in the public school system could be a disservice to the boy. He was far too bright to waste his time playing dodgeball and making paper-clip holders.

Maybe he'd look into finding a private school that could develop the potential that was obviously there.

The next moment, he forced himself to pull back. One step at a time, Chris silently warned himself. First they needed to get Joel into a school, *then* he could look into someplace better.

Not your problem, he reminded himself. If Jewel was successful, Joel would be turned over to his father and Ray could handle the boy's education. He had a life waiting for him, Chris reminded himself.

The thought left him feeling oddly hollow.

"She's here!" Joel suddenly declared with no small measure of enthusiasm.

Chris hadn't seen or heard anything to indicate that Jewel had arrived. "So now you have x-ray vision?" he teased the boy.

"No, I heard her car," Joel tossed over his shoulder as he rushed to the front door.

"Okay, no x-ray vision, superhearing," Chris amended under his breath. Because, heaven knew, he hadn't heard the car—or any car—approaching. But Joel obviously had. Since he had told Joel not to open the door to strangers, the boy went through the motions of looking out the window beside the door to make sure that it was Jewel coming up the walk. It was.

Jewel's index finger had barely made contact with the doorbell before the front door was swinging open. The next moment, she found herself looking down at Joel's beaming face.

"Boy, you certainly are excited about registering for school." She laughed as the small arms went around her hips in a greeting hug. Her hand tightened around the cell phone she was holding to keep from dropping it. The call to her mother had almost made her late.

"No, about seeing you," Joel corrected, pulling her into the house.

At that moment, she thought, Joel was every bit the five-year-old. She put away her phone and paused to smooth down his ruffled hair. Out of the corner of her eye, she saw Chris approaching them and nodded a greeting. "Hi."

"Hi." The turquoise jacket and skirt made her look like a businesswoman. *A sexy businesswoman,* he thought, then pushed the idea away before it could run off with him. "Any luck locating Ray?" he asked, needing something to fill the quiet.

She shook her head as she slipped her arm around Joel's shoulders. "Sorry, not yet."

It made no sense to Chris why her words prompted a feeling of relief within him, but now wasn't the time to explore that. He merely nodded at the information and said, "We'd better get going. The appointment's for eight-thirty."

Joel looked up at Jewel rather than him. "I'm ready."

She smiled at the boy. "Yes, you certainly are." She struggled to resist the urge to ruffle the hair she'd just smoothed down. "Let's go," she coaxed. Glancing over her shoulder at Chris as they walked out, she asked, "I'll drive. Okay?"

It made no difference to him. He wasn't one of those men who felt his car was an extension of his persona. It was just a means of getting from one place to another.

"Fine with me." As he approached her vehicle, he noted the new addition in the backseat. "You've got a child seat." Pausing, he looked from the seat to her. "You bought that?"

She opened the rear passenger door behind the driver's seat. "Had to if I'm going to be taking Joel anywhere. It's the law." Something that she had become aware of only yesterday. Before then, there had been no reason for her to pay attention to rules pertaining to children in cars. "Kids five and under have to sit in the back in a child seat—no matter how bright they are," she added with a wink at the boy. She nodded toward the seat. "Why don't you get in, Joel?"

He looked a little uncertain as he climbed in and shifted around until he was comfortable. "Where does this go?" he wanted to know, holding up the end of his seat belt.

"First we buckle you into the seat, then we put this around the seat," she explained, securing first the belt that came with the car seat, then the one that came with the car. "It's to keep you safe," she added as Joel looked down at the belts. She couldn't quite read his expression, but she could guess. Most kids didn't like restraints.

"How much do I owe you?" Chris asked as soon as he got in next to her.

Buckling up herself, she started up the car. "You mean the bill up until now?"

She'd quoted him a per diem rate, saying that it remained constant unless there were added expenses. She hadn't mentioned any of the latter so he was fairly confident he knew what that tally was.

"No, I mean, for the child seat," he clarified.

The seat was something she'd taken it upon herself to get. She wasn't about to charge him for it, not unless he wanted her to buy one for his car, too.

"It's okay. I've been meaning to get one." It was a lie, but it was a small one and in the larger scheme of things, Jewel felt she could be forgiven.

The thoughtful look on Chris's face bordered on a frown. "You have?"

"I'm thinking of expanding my clientele to include kids." The deadpan tone was so convincing that he almost believed her before he realized that she was pulling his leg. After a moment, the grin gave her away. "You never know when one of those things can come in handy. I plan on keeping it so, no," she told him, driving down the through street and out of the development, "you don't owe me anything."

He wasn't all that sure about that. She was helping him with Joel, putting herself out and doing things that he was fairly certain weren't part of her job description. Contrary to what she said, he owed her. A lot.

But, for now, he made no comment, merely nodding his head in response. Some things you couldn't settle up by writing a check.

* * *

"You just blew him away," Jewel declared a little less than two hours later as they were returning to her car. It was obvious when they arrived at Los Naranjos Elementary School that the principal, Dr. Randall Taylor, had very low expectations of the little boy who hardly spoke above a whisper when he was introduced. That soon changed as Joel read clearly and confidently from a third-grade reader.

Opening the rear door, she waited for Joel to climb onto his seat. "I don't think he's ever met anyone as bright as you before, Joel."

Looking down at the boy's face, she had a feeling that flattery was something new to him. He was absorbing her words like the drought-parched earth taking in the first rain in a very long time.

"You think I made a mistake, turning down his offer to have Joel skip a grade." It wasn't really a question Chris posed as he got into the car again. He had a feeling that he knew the answer.

He was wrong.

"I did for about five minutes," Jewel admitted. "But initially I didn't think it through. Now that I have, I realize that you're right." Starting the car, she paused to look at him before she released the brake. "You're probably speaking from experience, aren't you?" The fact that he didn't deny it spoke volumes. "How many grades did you skip?"

Chris shrugged. "Doesn't matter." Then, as she pulled out of the parking spot, he decided that there was no reason to keep the matter to himself. He wanted her to understand. "Two."

She thought as much. There'd been a look on his face when he politely thanked the principal for the suggestion, opting instead for a normal scholastic route for Joel for the time being, that told her there was a reason behind Chris's position. "Two different times, or all at once?"

"All at once." The laugh was self-depreciating, devoid of any humor. "Bad enough being the smartest kid in the class. When you're also the youngest by a couple of years…"

Chris didn't finish. He didn't have to. She had a vivid imagination and could certainly fill in the blanks.

She didn't attempt to hide her sympathy. "Must have been pretty rough for you."

There were times when pity and sympathy were difficult to separate. He wanted neither. He shrugged indifferently. "Could have been easier."

And he was trying to protect Joel from having to go through that, she thought. Rather than getting caught up with the academics of it all, trying to push his nephew to the outer limits of his abilities, Chris had wound up being more concerned with the boy's adjustment to the situation.

Well, well, well, Jewel thought, you learned something every day. Christopher Culhane was a good man. Better than she'd first guessed.

Joel spoke up suddenly. "This isn't the way home," he observed, watching the streets that whizzed by his window. "Are we going to the beach like you said?" he asked hopefully.

"Even better," Jewel responded, sparing just a second to look over her shoulder at the boy. "I have a surprise for you."

"What is it?" Joel wanted to know, eagerness and excitement pulsing in his voice.

"Well, if I told you, then it wouldn't be a surprise, now, would it?" Jewel asked, struggling to keep a straight face.

"No, ma'am. I guess not," Joel responded solemnly. Despite his resignation, his excitement was evident just below the surface.

Seeing life through the eyes of a child brought an optimistic sheen to everything, she thought. She'd almost forgotten what that had felt like. She had Joel to thank for reminding her.

Joel didn't have long to wait.

Jewel pulled up in her mother's driveway, and even before she turned off the ignition, her mother was coming out of the house, her arms opened wide in greeting.

She had to have been watching at the window, Jewel guessed. Some things never changed. She remembered her mother keeping vigil like that when she'd first started dating.

If the smile on Cecilia Parnell's subtly made-up face had been any wider, she would have had to rent a body double to accommodate the rest of it, Jewel thought, turning off the engine. She got out of the car and opened the rear passenger door.

"Remember the ladies who came to your mom's funeral?" Jewel asked him as she helped Joel out of the restraining belts. "Well, they thought you were so much fun to play with, they asked me if you could come by so they could have a rematch."

Although the thought obviously appealed to Joel, the shift in his expression told her that he saw a small problem with that.

"But I didn't bring the video game," he told Jewel in a whisper.

Jewel struggled to suppress her grin as she pulled the handheld player out of her purse. "But I did."

Joel eagerly took possession of the game, his eyes dancing. "You think of everything!" he declared happily.

The boy filled her with joy, Jewel thought, absorbing his happiness as it radiated out. She couldn't help glancing back at Chris. "This is one great kid."

She'd get no argument from him. Chris was becoming convinced of the same thing himself. He watched as Joel ran up to the trio of women and each took her turn hugging him. Chris noted that his nephew no longer just stoically took the displays of affection as if he were afraid they would vanish at any moment, but returned them, as well.

It looked as if Joel was set for the next few hours. Chris slanted a look toward the woman responsible for it all. "Does this mean I have time to go over to the university?"

"That's what it means. C'mon," she beckoned, already reopening the driver's side door. "I'll drive you back to Rita's so you can pick up your car."

"Take your time, you two," Cecilia called after them. She already had Joel under her wing, literally and otherwise. "We want to enjoy Joel's company. You do the same with each other."

Jewel shut her eyes for a second, gathering strength. Wondering if anyone had ever died from humiliation. "See you later, Mother," she called out tersely.

As Chris buckled up and she started the car, she debated about whether to let the matter go or to say something to apologize.

Ultimately, she decided that the "hint" her mother had sent their way was much too blatant to ignore. "Sorry about that," she murmured, starting down the road.

He looked at her quizzically, apparently not following her line of thought. "About what?"

He was just being polite. It was like saying that he wasn't aware of the elephant in the room. "My mother and her parting comment."

It took him a second to make the connection. "Oh. That." The smile on his lips was a tolerant one. To him the apology was entirely unnecessary. "From what I gather—and I have no firsthand experience with this— Cecilia was just being a mother. She wants you to be happy."

She wanted to ask him what he meant by saying that he had no firsthand experience. Was *this* referring to a meddling mother, or something else? But she decided that perhaps he wasn't up to probing right now. She let it ride.

"What she wants is for me to be married," Jewel corrected.

His broad shoulders rose and fell beneath his jacket. "Maybe to her that's one and the same thing."

"Very astute of you," she acknowledged, a smile playing on her lips. "My mother, bless her, grew up in a completely different generation when the words, *'til death do us part* actually meant something. Now, if they mean anything, it's only because one spouse has killed the other." She bit back a sigh as she decided not to race through a swiftly changing yellow light.

Chris studied her profile as they waited for the light to change again. "And I thought I had dark thoughts."

"They're not dark thoughts," she protested, shifting her foot onto the gas pedal. "That's reality. I admit that, because of my line of work, I get to see a bigger share of disgruntled married couples who want nothing more than to be rid of one another than most people. But even if I didn't see them, they'd still be there," she pointed out. "If a tree falls in the forest, it still makes a noise even if there's no one to hear it." She used the familiar saying to make her point for her.

"Marriage doesn't mean what it used to. People don't stick together through thick and thin anymore. At the first sign of unrest or trouble, they're out of there, shedding mates like snakes shed skin." She hated this particular fact of life, but that didn't make it any less true. "My mother and her friends were a lot luckier. They didn't just marry good men, they married 'forever.'" Jewel blew out a breath. She was letting the subject get to her, and Chris was a captive audience. She shouldn't be subjecting him to this. "I'm sorry, I didn't mean to preach—or vent."

"I think venting probably fits the situation better. But you know," he hypothesized, "statistically speaking, if fifty percent of marriages fail, that means that fifty percent of them succeed. You strike me as someone who's pretty determined. If you were to marry someone, it would be forever. You'd make damn sure of it."

Whether he realized it or not, he'd just succeeded in raising her spirits. "That's a very nice sentiment, Chris."

He didn't like being thanked and that was where this was headed. He offered a disclaimer. "Just an observation," he replied.

She caught another red light. At this rate, it was going to take forever to get him to his car, she thought. "You have trouble accepting gratitude, don't you?"

He pretended not to know what she was talking about. "Was that what that was?"

"That's what that was," she confirmed. The next moment, she turned a corner then pointed toward the house on the right. "We're here."

He looked out. "So we are. By the way, what time am I supposed to pick up Joel?"

"That's entirely up to you. I'm sure the later you come by, the happier my mother and her friends will be." Parking in the driveway, Jewel pulled up the hand brake. The engine was still running as she paused to let Chris out. With her free hand, she dug through her purse, searching for her cell phone in order to check something on her schedule.

Except that she couldn't. No matter where she felt

around, she couldn't seem to locate the phone. "Damn, I know it's in here somewhere."

Chris paused by the car door. "What is?"

"My cell phone." She shook her purse a little, thinking it might surface.

"You had it out in the house," he recalled.

Right. Now she remembered. Jewel sighed. "And left it there."

"C'mon, I'll let you in," he offered.

Maybe it was her, she thought as she turned off the engine and got out, but for one moment, the words seemed to have the ring of a prophecy about them.

Chapter Twelve

The moment Chris unlocked the door for her, Jewel hurried inside the house.

Her cell phone was exactly where she thought it would be. Right on top of the coffee table where she'd put it when Joel ran up to hug her.

"Got it," she announced, putting it into the zippered compartment of her purse.

Slipping the purse's strap onto her shoulder, she glanced in Chris's direction, trying to gauge his thoughts. She didn't want him to think that she was scatterbrained. If he thought she had trouble locating her cell phone, he might have doubts about her ability to track down Joel's father.

"In case you're wondering," she told him, "I don't usually misplace my phone."

He shook his head. "Didn't think you did," he

answered matter-of-factly. His eyes slid over her curves slowly. Right now, his thoughts were miles away from mundane things like misplaced cell phones. Or even getting back to work.

Right now, all his thoughts were centered on her.

On what it felt like to have her against him. That kiss the other day had set a great many questions in motion for him. Questions that would never have any answers, unless...

Jewel shifted slightly, a restless feeling suffusing her mind, body and soul. It was time for her to leave, she told herself. There were a couple of resources she needed to tap before she could put out more feelers.

Yet she wasn't moving, wasn't going out the door or even turning in that direction. Her eyes had met his and the moment they did, a nervous anticipation skittered around inside of her.

Because silence was stretching out between them, swallowing seconds, Jewel searched for something to say. Anything, no matter how inane. "Bet you can't wait to get back inside a college classroom."

He'd almost said "yes," but that would have just been an automatic answer, not a truthful one. A week ago, it would have been, but not anymore. A week ago, the University of Bedford constituted his whole life and he'd been content with that. At least, he'd *thought* he was content with that.

But now, completely against his will, his horizon had been expanded.

If he said "yes," then that would have been the end of it. She'd walk away to do whatever it was she was going to do and he'd drive over to the university, hours ahead of schedule.

He didn't want an end to it. Didn't want her to walk away. Not even for a moment.

"That's not a hundred percent true," Chris heard himself saying.

She wasn't quite sure she understood what he was saying. There were a number of conflicting signals going out, confusing the hell out of her. "I thought you lived and breathed teaching—when you weren't writing," Jewel tacked on.

"So did I," he freely admitted. He found himself taking another step toward her. And then another. It was almost as if he had no choice in the matter. "Looks like we both might be wrong."

"Oh?" She could feel her very breath backing up in her lungs. Or was she just holding it, waiting? "I don't think I quite understand."

Chris laughed softly, as if the sound was only intended for him. "That makes two of us." With effort, he tried to wall off his emotions, tried to back away. But he remained where he was, far too aware of her proximity, far too aware of *her* for his own good.

Or hers.

"I'm keeping you." He was doing his best not to let this happen. "You have an appointment."

The words left her lips in slow motion. "Actually, I don't." She hadn't been definite in her plans, telling her contact only that she would be dropping by some time on Monday. That left it wide-open, which was just the way she liked it. Free to come and go as she pleased.

So why wasn't she going? "But you have a class," she reminded him.

"Not until three o'clock." He glanced at his watch, although he was already well aware of the time. "It's only ten forty-five."

The corners of her mouth curved slightly. "With that much time, you could walk to the campus."

"Or do something else entirely," he countered quietly.

Her mouth went utterly dry. So dry she was surprised that she managed to push the single word out. "What?" Her heart was hammering so hard, it was about to break the sound barrier. Cries of "Mayday" echoed in her brain.

Chris gently cupped her cheek with his hand. Time froze and completely stood still. Nothing moved but her pounding heart, which was threatening to vibrate right out of her chest.

As he began to lower his mouth to hers, she had the answer to her question. "Oh, that," she murmured breathlessly.

His lips were a fraction of an inch from hers when her response stopped him. *Was* he assuming too much? "I can back away if you—"

Chris never got a chance to finish.

He thought he heard Jewel warn, "Don't you dare," but he wasn't sure because the next moment, her hands were framing the sides of his face and *she* was pulling *him* into a kiss.

Pulling him into her space. Into her world.

Her lips locked on his as she rose up on her toes so

that they could both feel the full impact of the heated contact.

When she finally drew back to allow them both to catch their breath, he did his best to try to keep the moment light, even while his head was spinning and his blood surged madly through his veins.

"Is that because you found your phone?" Though he did his best not to show it, he ran out of breath by the next to the last word.

"As good an excuse as any," she told him, fighting back a grin. "I was always taught to celebrate the little things."

Damn but he wanted her.

None of this was making any sense to him. He wasn't acting like himself. But there was no going back, no pulling away.

He took her into his arms, drawing her closer. "By all means, let's celebrate."

And that was how it began.

How her entrance into a brand-new, shining world she had never quite experienced before started. There'd been other men, although not nearly as many as she had pretended, but never once did the ground disappear beneath her feet, never once could she recall being filled with an anticipation she couldn't really control.

And never once, at the very end, when the magic and the starlight had passed and it was all over, had disappointment *not* been hovering somewhere in the wings, waiting to pounce and overtake her.

Disappointment didn't even put a toe into the water this time, didn't cast a *hint* of a shadow.

What was there was fire, heat, a dizzying sense of satisfaction even as the next bombshell had already begun to form.

Again.

She'd never lost her sense of orientation before, never felt so excited, so overwhelmed that she completely lost track of the sequence of events.

Oh, she knew they'd started out fully dressed in the living room and wound up stripped, panting and sealed together, sweaty and passionate, in the master bedroom. But how was unclear.

What she *did* remember were sounds and sensations and the feel of his hands, surprisingly strong, yet incredibly gentle, running along the length of her body. But if she were asked to verbally re-create what had happened, moment by moment, there was no way she could.

Urgency had been her companion, cheering her on as she reached one plateau after another, always believing that this was the end of it, only to discover that there was more. More sensations to absorb, more crescendos to savor, each of them echoing hard throughout her entire body.

With his hand on the Bible, vowing to speak the truth and nothing but, Chris couldn't have said what had come over him. Why, when he should have been reaching for his worn briefcase, he found himself reaching for her instead. But suddenly, the need to be alone with her, the desire to make love with this woman who was so completely different from anyone he'd ever known, had been so overpowering that he knew that this was something he couldn't even *begin* to ignore.

Chris had never been one to seize hold of life before. Instead, he had gone along his quiet path, giving himself up to science. He liked things that made sense, no matter how long it took for him to arrive at the conclusion.

This, this made no sense at all.

But it felt wonderful.

He couldn't remember ever feeling this alive before. Or, he realized as he gave in to another surge of impulse and brushed his lips along the tantalizing length of her body, feeling this happy.

Unable to hold himself in check any longer, Chris drew his body up along Jewel's until his eyes were looking down into hers.

And then he took her.

Or she him.

He wasn't certain of the order, all he knew was that he couldn't ignore the demands of the rhythm that had taken him prisoner, holding on to him tightly. The rhythm echoed faster and faster until, suddenly, he was propelled into another world where two people became one and nothing else made sense but that.

He was vaguely aware of her crying out, and the sound vibrated in his head even as the heated embrace of euphoria receded inch by cooling inch from around his body.

Chris became aware that his arms were wrapped around her, as if that sole act could stave off the onslaught of reality. He wanted the feeling of euphoria to remain forever.

But even as he thought it, the feeling was breaking

up, expiring like the bubbles in a bubble bath after their time was past.

"I didn't hurt you, did I?" she heard him ask, his warm breath brushing up against her skin. Heating it all over again.

"I don't know," she admitted. "This is the first out-of-body experience I've ever had." And she fervently hoped it wasn't going to be the last. She wasn't naive enough to believe that this was the beginning of the rest of her life, but she was hopeful enough to pray that there were a few more moments like this left for her before she and Chris went their separate ways.

Raising her head, she leaned her arm across his chest and then rested her chin against it.

Her eyes danced as she deadpanned, "Was it something I said?"

He'd been afraid that he'd gone too far, presumed too much. Hearing the teasing question brought a sense of relief to him.

"No," he answered honestly. "It was something you did."

If she'd somehow triggered this wondrous experience, she needed to know. That way she could do it again. "What?" she pressed.

"You were," he replied. When she looked at him, puzzled, he repeated, "You just were."

Jewel needed more of a hint than that. She ran her fingertip along his lips. She was arousing him. She could see it.

"Were what?" she pressed.

"You. You were you. And magnificent," he whispered

just before he drew her head down to his. Her mouth down to his.

The lovemaking began all over again, with even more pulsating excitement this time because each knew what was waiting for them just around the corner. And because time, ever an enemy, was growing short. Life was waiting for them just outside the door.

They made the most of the moment.

Late that afternoon, when Chris arrived to pick Joel up from Cecilia's house, he saw that Jewel's car was parked at the curb.

She was here.

A dozen or more feelings instantly sprang up, assaulting him from every angle. It had been difficult enough to keep his mind on his lesson plan as he stood at the front of his classroom. If he forgot a word or two, or missed a beat, he knew it would be attributed to his having lost his sister. All his classes had been informed by the substituting professor why he hadn't been there for the past few sessions.

But how was he going to pretend that nothing monumental had happened between the two of them when he walked into Cecilia's house and caught his first glimpse of Jewel?

And his second glimpse and his third?

How was he going to pretend that he wanted to do something other than sweep her into his arms and start the lovemaking process all over again?

He felt as if someone had slipped into his body and transformed him.

Jewel could feel the pulse in her throat going haywire—or at least it seemed that way—the moment she saw him take command of the room.

She did her best to appear nonchalant when Chris walked into the living room after her mother had opened the front door to admit him.

Her best was not good enough.

Maybe this was a bad idea. Maybe she should have gone straight to his sister's house to give him a progress report. Encountering him here, under the watchful eyes of her mother and her mother's fellow yentas, the same day that Chris had made the earth move for her might not have been the smartest thing she had ever done.

Even if she could exercise steely control over herself, her mother, bless her, had a sixth sense when it came to the vibes given off by a man and a woman.

And Maizie was even worse. The only one who wasn't as tuned in to those things—and was more thoughtful about making her suspicions public—was Theresa. Although, Jewel reconsidered, not to hear Kate tell it.

She forced a smile to her lips and tried to sound as distant as possible as she told Chris, "I just wanted to let you know that I think I might be onto something."

The look on Chris's face told her that he wholeheartedly agreed. That, as far as his opinion went, she most definitely *was* onto something.

She was quick to set him straight. "About the location of Joel's father," Jewel stressed, lowering her voice.

"Oh. Good." The first word reflected that he was still somewhat stunned to see her. The second word so lacked feeling and enthusiasm that she thought he hadn't really heard her. That *was* why he'd hired her, wasn't it? To find the boy's real father.

"I have to follow it up," she continued, "but it seems to be the first solid lead I have."

He remembered her saying something about tracing the man through his IRS filings. Was that what she'd done? And why didn't he feel a sense of relief or happiness at the thought of locating Joel's father? This was what he'd wanted. To pass the obligation of taking care of another human being onto someone else.

Had his wiring gone so far off-kilter today that nothing made sense to him?

"Well, that's good news, isn't it?" Theresa asked slowly, looking from Jewel to Chris and then back again. It was obvious by their expressions that neither of them saw this as particularly good news. Theresa smiled as she exchanged glances with Cecilia.

"Yes. Of course. Good news." Chris was parroting the words. Who would have ever thought that such a small woman could upend his world? And at his age. It just didn't seem possible.

And yet, it was true.

He looked strange, Jewel thought. As if all four cylinders of his engine weren't firing correctly. "Is something wrong?" she asked him, concerned.

"No, nothing," he assured her a little too quickly. "I'd better get Joel home," Chris said suddenly. "He's got a big day tomorrow."

Apparently oblivious to the conversation going on around him up until this moment, Joel's head snapped up. His small eyes darted from his uncle to his new—and only—best friend.

"Jewel?"

There were so many things she heard in Joel's small, reedy voice. It didn't take much for her to know that what he needed most was reassurance. "Sure, I can come with you tomorrow to drop you off."

He didn't look the least bit surprised that she had read his mind. "And pick me up?"

Chris looked on, somewhat surprised by the exchange.

"And pick you up," Jewel confirmed with a wide smile. "And in between, you're going to have a great time," she promised the boy, putting her arm around the small shoulders. She slanted a look toward his temporary guardian. "Isn't he, Uncle Chris?"

Chris's eyes met hers over the boy's head. "Absolutely."

One glance at the boy's face told them that Joel was far from convinced.

She had her work cut out for her, Jewel thought. But she worked best under pressure. "Want me to come over tonight?" she asked the boy.

Both Joel and his uncle said, "Yes," their voices overlapping.

Jewel grinned. Her eyes went from the grown man who'd lit up her world to the little boy who lit up whenever he saw her. She deliberately avoided looking in her mother's direction—or the direction of either of the other two women. She wasn't up to dealing with their knowing expressions.

"You got it," she told the two males in the room.

Unable to avoid it, out of the corner of her eye she glanced toward her mother and saw the smug, satisfied look. It was enough to make her want to shout, "It's not what you're thinking!"

But, unfortunately, it was.

It was *exactly* what her mother was thinking. And that, truthfully, was the only fly in the ointment for her because, although she dearly loved the woman who had given her life, Jewel knew what Cecilia Parnell was capable of. If she grazed the ball just once, it encouraged her to take a thousand swings at bat. And even though they might all turn out to be misses, her mother would keep on swinging until she had another hit, however minor, to her credit.

Her only salvation, Jewel thought, was that once Chris was history, as he surely would be, she would tell her mother that there was nothing between them except for Joel.

But even as she thought it, she had a feeling her mother wouldn't believe her.

Chapter Thirteen

Before the week was out, Chris felt that he had, in essence, reclaimed his life. He was back teaching at the university and he was once again working on the college textbook. But life was not without its surprises.

He discovered, much to his amazement, that what had once sustained him and given him purpose now just wasn't enough. He looked back over his years in the academic world and was mystified that he had ever thought that his life was full. It wasn't. There was an emptiness at the core, an emptiness that he now realized he had unconsciously tried to ignore by filling his time with work. Perpetual work.

He published papers, did research and occasionally volunteered to take over classes for vacationing fellow science professors. All, he now knew, in order to avoid coming face-to-face with the truth: Man could not live by job devotion alone.

There was a need for balance that could only be arrived at by filling that all-consuming hole with family. With the fulfillment that being needed on a personal basis brought. Providing a home and emotional support for his nephew had made all that clear to him.

But even being both mother and father—temporarily, he reminded himself—for the boy did not sufficiently fill up the hole. For that to happen, there had to be something more.

There had to be Jewel.

She completed the unit.

Completed him.

Even as he thought that, Chris turned to face Jewel, silently warning himself not to get too attached to any of it. That at any moment, everything could change in a heartbeat. The way it had with Rita's death. Except that this time, it would be Joel's departure that would bring about the change. The boy would be leaving if his father were found. As would Jewel, because finding Ray was what she'd signed on for. There would be no reason for her to keep meeting with him once that was accomplished.

Unless she wanted to.

Chris sighed, staring up at the darkened ceiling. He was a novice at this, at keeping the fragile pseudo–family unit together, alive and well. One misstep and it would all be over, shattered beyond repair.

He now knew what a tightrope walker had to feel like, trying to inch his way from one end of the rope to the other without falling. Without losing everything. The very thought made his gut tighten. Almost to the point where he couldn't breathe.

Chris shifted in the bed he'd commandeered—Rita's bed—and slowly turned back to the woman beside him. The woman, partly to present her reports verbally, partly in response to Joel's perpetual requests to see her, had taken to coming over every evening after five o'clock. They would all have dinner together and then they would take turns, when he didn't have papers to grade, helping Joel with his homework.

Chris smiled to himself. The first time that happened, he'd expressed surprise that there actually *was* homework in kindergarten, but obviously the school believed in working with young minds right from the start. And that was a good thing.

So one of them would help the boy with his homework and thus a pattern was created. First they'd all spend time together, then after Joel was tucked into bed and read to until he fell asleep, Jewel and he would carve out their own private heaven, making love with a passion that said things that neither of them had yet ventured to voice aloud: that they knew this was just temporary. That they were making the most of the time they had together. Storing memories for the time when they would no longer *be* together.

She could feel Chris looking at her. Studying her. Jewel turned into him, her naked body brushing up against his.

Odd how quickly she'd grown so comfortable around him, she thought. There was no awkwardness in the silences that occasionally occurred between them, no sense of urgency to fill the air with conversation.

But even though there was no awkwardness, she sensed that there was something bothering him. Something he was having difficulty putting into words.

"Something on your mind you want to talk about?" Jewel coaxed softly.

He was beginning to think she was a mind reader. She always seemed to know when he was holding things back. "What makes you say that?"

Jewel raised herself up on her elbow and ran her fingertips lightly along the furrow that had formed between his eyebrows. The same kind of furrow that Joel had when he was thinking.

"You're pensive," she told him. "As if you don't know how to phrase whatever it is that you're wrestling with."

That was as good a summation as any. Chris sighed. "Maybe I don't."

"Just spit it out," she encouraged, then teased, "There won't be any points off for bad grammar, I promise."

He wasn't getting anywhere silently chewing on this. Making up his mind, he plunged in. "You haven't found Ray yet."

Was that what this was about? That so far, despite her best efforts, she hadn't been able to produce Joel's father? She hadn't given up by a long shot.

"We're not out of options yet," she told Chris. "One of the people I know is putting me in touch with—"

"Maybe we should stop looking." Now, that surprised her.

She didn't understand. Chris had been so adamant about locating Joel's father when he'd first hired her. Not that much time had gone by. What was going on? Why had he changed his mind?

"Why would we do that?"

He gave her reasons, going about it as if he were proving a theorem. "Look at it logically. If Ray had wanted to be part of Joel's life, he would have found a way to stay in contact with him. Phone calls, birthday cards, postcards if he's traveling. Something," he emphasized. "After all, Joel's his son. That's supposed to mean something. Instead, there hasn't been anything in three years. Three *years*. For all intents and purposes, it's like Ray just dropped off the face of the earth. Maybe he doesn't *want* to be found."

It made sense. But all this was true when he hired her. She had a feeling that there was more.

"What else?" she prodded.

Chris slowly blew out a breath before answering. One hand under his head, he tucked the other around her and brought Jewel closer to him.

"Bringing Ray back after all this time will just toss Joel's life into chaos again. Ray may be his father, but he's a complete stranger to Joel. It would be like putting him into a foster home. I can help supplement his education and, in case you haven't noticed, the kid lights up like a Christmas tree every time he sees you. Joel's happy now, possibly for the first time in his life, and I don't think I have the right to spoil that for him. To shake things up for him by bringing his father into it."

He paused. Was he being selfish or altruistic? He

wasn't really sure. All he knew was that he didn't think that changing things again so soon after Rita's death was a good idea.

"Maybe we should just let sleeping dogs lie," Chris said.

"Maybe," Jewel acknowledged. She knew he didn't want to hear this, but it had to be put out on the table. "But what happens if that sleeping dog wakes up and wanders into your lives?"

Puzzled, he turned into her. "What?"

She spelled it out for him. "What if Ray comes back on his own for whatever reason and finds out that Rita's dead and his son's being raised by the brother-in-law he's always felt inferior to?"

Her assumption caught him off guard. He looked at her, confused. "What makes you think he felt inferior to me?"

"Things I picked up on while trying to locate Ray." Jewel sat up to look at him, ignoring the fact that she was nude from the waist up. "We might never be able to find Ray, but we have to continue trying as long as there are still avenues to pursue." She didn't go into details, but she was fairly sure that she was on the right track. "Because if we just call it all off, I guarantee you're going to spend the rest of your parental life looking over your shoulder, expecting Ray to just show up one day and take Joel from you, maybe just out of spite. Trust me. You don't want to have to live like that."

Chris slowly shook his head. "No. You're right. I don't."

And because it was the middle of the night and

nothing could be done about it one way or another right now, he set the matter aside and focused on her. On the lightly bronzed beauty sitting up next to him and looking like a goddess.

He felt his gut tightening all over again. Tightening out of need and radiating far-reaching fingers of desire all through him.

"How did you get to be so wise?" he wanted to know, slipping his hands on either side of her waist.

She grinned. "Dumb luck most of the time. Instincts make up the rest of it," she added.

Chris was now lightly skimming his palms and fingers along her waist and inching his way up to the sides of her breasts. Desires and needs flooded through her, making her ache for him all over again, even though they had already made love, not once but twice. And only a few minutes ago she'd thought she was too exhausted to breathe.

But from out of nowhere a fresh, new burst of energy emerged, drenching her and energizing her all at the same time.

Leaning over, she brushed her lips lightly against his. Once, twice and then again, each pass lingering just a second longer than the last.

He cupped the back of her head, bringing her closer to keep her from ending the kiss too soon.

The kiss deepened.

As he savaged and savored her mouth, Chris could feel his self-control ebbing away. She could reduce him to a mass of passions so quickly he hardly knew how it happened.

Only that it did.

He'd never known anyone like Jewel before and, most likely, never would again. She was an anomaly he couldn't begin to understand. Being who he was, he promised himself that someday he would unravel this enigma that was Jewel Parnell.

But not tonight.

Tonight there would only be a third round of lovemaking. There was no room for anything else. Tomorrow with its cold reality was still light-years away from here, he promised himself.

With a swift movement, Chris shifted their positions and suddenly, she was the one on the bottom and he on top. Moving his body in a gentle, familiar rhythm, he paid homage to every soft, pliable, damp inch of her, grazing her body with his fingers and his mouth.

Starting a fire that mere water couldn't begin to put out.

She shouldn't be doing this. Sleeping with Chris had long ceased being about just enjoying herself and scratching an "itch" that was distracting her. She was sinking into that place where she *needed* this to keep on functioning. Needed to have this man make love with her. Needed to feel his lips on hers, needed the wondrous high that only he seemed capable of creating for her each and every time a climax shuddered through her.

It was that old catch-22. The more she made love with him, the more she wanted to make love with him. She knew she needed to stop, to walk away while she still could…

Who was she kidding? That window had long since shut. She *couldn't* walk away.

And yet, she knew she couldn't stay, either. To stay would be to invite the tarnish to come, as it did with each relationship that was out there.

Better to have all this live on in her memory, perfect and wonderful, than to have it disintegrate right in front of her, turning sour the way she had seen so many relationships do, time after time.

If she continued like this, all she was doing was setting herself up for a fall. For an all-consuming, crashing disappointment.

Nothing lasted forever. Or even came close.

But, oh, it was so hard to be strong when the fire inside her belly threatened to eat her alive.

Later. She'd think about it later.

When she could think.

Because right now, Chris's very presence was blotting out her ability to form coherent thoughts. Even short ones.

There was only one cure for that. And it was temporary at best.

Threading her arms around his neck, Jewel arched her hips to admit him and gave herself up to the revelry that hovered such a short distance away, waiting to swallow her up.

"So how's it going?" Kate asked breathlessly. Two steps ahead of Jewel, she had just taken a seat at the small table she'd commandeered for their semi-regular get-together at the coffee shop that was located across the street from Nikki's hospital.

Every week or two, she, Jewel and Nikki tried to meet at least for coffee to touch base with one another. But a last-minute patient emergency had Nikki calling to beg off today, so it was just Jewel and Kate this time around. Until recently, they'd used these meetings to commiserate about their marriage-minded, interfering, matchmaking mothers. But of late, the lament had proven to be no longer necessary, since two of them were now, much to their mothers' unending joy, engaged to be married.

Kate set down the two coffees she was carrying and slid one across the short length of the table to Jewel.

Her eyes were dancing as she said, "I hear Aunt Cecilia sent you a man you couldn't refuse."

"Who told you that?" Jewel asked sharply. Hands wrapped tightly around the container, she was about to take a sip but stopped dead at Kate's question.

"I don't have a 'single' informant," Kate told her. "Like everything else, it came in threes. Aunt Cecilia, Aunt Maizie and my mother, all of whom have declared, separately and together, that this guy—Christopher Culhane is it?—is the 'perfect catch.'" She took a healthy swallow before leaning in to Jewel. "Your mother even showed me a picture of him." Kate smiled, pleased for Jewel. "He's very good-looking." She winked at her friend. "If I wasn't so crazy in love with Jackson, I might have even Indian-wrestled you for this guy."

Jewel was still digesting the previous part of Kate's statement. "A picture? Where did my mother get a picture of him?"

A horrifying scenario presented itself to Jewel. Her mother posing Chris like some artist's model in a nude sculpting class. She could feel her cheeks heating and picked up the cup again. She could blame the shift in her skin tone on the hot coffee if Kate noticed.

"Actually," Kate amended, "she showed me a page out of the University of Bedford's last yearbook. They had the professors listed separately. A physics professor." She gave a low, appreciative whistle. "I must say I'm impressed."

She had to nip this in the bud now. The last thing she wanted was for either one of her almost-married best friends to come up and lavish pity on her once she and Chris went their separate ways—as they inevitably would sooner or later.

"There's no point in being impressed," Jewel told her dismissively. "There's nothing going on."

Jewel had a tell, an unconscious giveaway when she was lying to someone she cared about. A tic in her right cheek would start up. She knew it was all but dancing now.

Kate kept a straight face. "Oh?"

Jewel shrugged. She and Kate, as well as Nikki, had been friends since birth. Maybe even since conception. Keeping things from either of them had never been easy for her. She could hide the truth from her mother far more easily than she could from her friends.

So with a sigh she said, "Well, there's 'something' going on," she was referring to their nightly lovemaking sessions, "but there's nothing going on if you get my meaning."

"Possibly, in some alternate universe," Kate allowed, "but here, in this one... Huh?"

She spelled it out to Kate. "Okay, Chris's a hell of a lover, but you and I know that being a fantastic lover doesn't add up to 'forever.'"

Kate clearly wasn't about to dismiss the man that quickly. "It could, given other attributes."

But Jewel remained firm in her convictions. "I'm not going to set myself up for a fall, Kate. You and Nikki might have lucked out, but there's only so much luck out there to be had."

"It's not luck and you know it," Kate insisted. "A relationship—any relationship—takes hard work and determination and a real willingness to compromise. A lot," she underscored.

"All true," Jewel allowed, but she had a different perspective on the matter, one she'd learned from her long, tedious hours of surveillance. "However, all those heartbroken, cheated-on spouses who hire me, they thought they all had that extra-special relationship, too—until they suddenly had the rug pulled out from under them and landed hard on their bruised hearts."

"Then tack the rug down," Kate advised matter-of-factly. She reached across the table, putting her hand on top of Jewel's. "At the very least, Jewel, don't declare whatever it is that the two of you have going on dead while it's still got a breath of life left within it. I'd hate to see you miss out on something wonderful because you're afraid."

"I'm not afraid," Jewel protested with feeling.

Kate's pager went off. She glanced down at the

number on the tiny LCD screen. The moment she did, she rose to her feet. "Looks like I'm out of time, Jewel. They want me in court. Think about what I said," she requested with feeling. "Oh, by the way, the coffees are paid for," she tossed over her shoulder a second before she hurried out the door.

"I am *not* afraid," Jewel repeated with more feeling, saying the words to her friend's retreating back.

But she knew she was.

Chapter Fourteen

This definitely was *not* the reaction she'd expected.

Having moved heaven and three-quarters of the earth, reaching out to people she hadn't been in contact with for some time now—in some cases several years—Jewel had finally managed to pinpoint the location of Joel's father. Ray Johnson was currently living in Las Vegas under an assumed name and doubling as a dealer/bouncer at one of the lesser-known casinos.

She was fairly proud of herself for being able to track the man down by using the thumbprint on his California driver's license. He'd allowed that license to expire, but on a hunch she'd put the thumbprint into the system and run it through a number of different databases. While nothing came up in either the military service database or the one that listed felons across the country, a match kicked out in the database that kept prints on hand for everyone employed by the gaming industry in Nevada.

She'd remembered thinking that it was lucky for them that working at a casino required having your fingerprints taken.

Now it didn't seem to matter.

"What do you mean, forget it?" she asked Chris incredulously.

"Just that, forget it," he repeated. Thinking she might be afraid that he was going to renege on their initial arrangement, he added, "I'll pay you for your time and any extra expenses you might have incurred trying to locate Ray."

This really didn't make any sense to her. She remembered how eager he had been to get out from under the responsibility of caring for his nephew. "So you don't want me going to Las Vegas to bring this guy back?"

"No."

Even if he'd changed his mind about the responsibility portion, he knew that it was only right to let the man know what had happened. "I thought we already had this conversation," she said, addressing his back as he paced about the room.

It was late. Verifying her information had taken a while and she'd arrived here only in time to say goodnight to Joel. Consequently, bedtime had been stretched to the limit, but eventually, Joel fell asleep. And then she had dropped her bombshell.

"We did," he agreed.

She caught his hand to keep him from continuing to pace. It was like talking to a moving target at a shooting gallery. "And the outcome," she reminded Chris, "was that you agreed that I should keep on looking for Ray."

"That was when I didn't think you would find him," he confessed. He shouldn't have underestimated her. "Now that you have..." His voice trailed off for a moment, then he continued with conviction. "I don't think it's in Joel's best interest to have his father back in his life. Ray was short-tempered, argumentative and I'd call him dumb as a post, except I'd be insulting posts everywhere. If Joel goes to live with him, I guarantee that the boy will be put down every day of his life. He's already smarter than his father ever was and Ray doesn't like to feel inferior."

She stared at him, confused. "If you felt that way, why did you start this? Why did you have me even looking for the man?"

"Because I didn't think it through," he answered honestly, then owned up to something even more unflattering. "Because I was just thinking of myself. I wanted to get back to my life, to the way things were. Except that's not enough for me anymore," he admitted. "I like coming home and hearing Joel tell me about his day. It gives a whole new meaning to everything. I can nurture him," he said with feeling. "Ray, or whatever he's calling himself these days, can't. *Won't*," he underscored.

She held her hands up to stop him from saying any more. "Hey, you're preaching to the choir here."

He was relieved to hear that. "Then we can just forget about this?"

Surprise shot through him when he saw her solemnly shake her head. "No."

He didn't understand why she was refusing his request. "But I thought you said you agreed with me."

"I do, but that doesn't mean that you can just forget about Ray—who, by the way, now goes by Dennis Carter," she interjected. "Because if we don't get a signed document from the man, saying he relinquishes all parental rights to Joel, the lovely world you're projecting in your head runs the very real risk of blowing up at any given moment—without warning."

She'd grabbed his attention right at the beginning. "A signed document?"

Jewel nodded. Tired from her long day, she sank down on the sofa. "That's what I said."

He was silent for a long moment, turning the matter over in his head. "Do you think Ray'll agree?" he finally asked.

She thought they had a very good shot at it. "From everything you've told me about the man, I think it's a safe bet. He sounds like a selfish jerk and it really bothered me that you were willing to just hand Joel over."

"Well, I'm not anymore," he emphasized. Rather than sit down next to her, he perched on the sofa's arm, restless. "But what if he doesn't sign away his rights? What if he decides, for whatever strange reason, to give fatherhood another shot? By going to him, we'll be letting him know where to find Joel."

She tried to assuage Chris's fears by using his own arguments on him. "As you said the other night, if he had been interested in getting back in touch with Joel, he would have tried to reach out to him at some point. An official document filed with the court will buy you peace of mind. I can have one of my friends—she's a family lawyer and, coincidentally, Theresa's daughter," Jewel interjected, "draw up the proper legal papers for you. We can be on the road tomorrow if you like."

He laughed shortly. "What I'd like," he told her, "would be to never have started this in the first place." He played the words back in his head and realized what was wrong with that path. "But, then, I wouldn't have met you, would I?"

Her smile was soft.

Jewel hadn't changed her mind about the situation. She knew what they had was only temporary, but she could certainly cherish it for all she was worth while it lasted.

"No," she agreed, "you wouldn't have."

Never one to count chickens before they had not only hatched but had also shed their downy fuzz and grown feathers, he still allowed himself a moment.

"I guess having to see Ray again is worth it." His eyes drifted over her, taking possession. "Especially considering what I got in the bargain." He laced his fingers through hers. "You said you think we can be on our way tomorrow?"

She nodded. "Just as soon as I have Kate draw up those papers for Ray to sign."

Chris had to admit, if only silently to himself, that he felt a little uneasy about getting in contact with Ray. The man might just decide to retain custody out of spite. But he knew that Jewel was right. This had to be done.

"Do it," he told her. "Get the necessary papers drawn up."

He sounded as if he were steeling himself off, she

thought. "You know, if you'd rather not have to deal with this character, I can go to Vegas as your representative. There's no need to put yourself through this if you don't want to."

But Chris was already shaking his head, turning down her offer before she finished.

"No. I need to see him, to make sure he understands that if he does take Joel, I'll be all over his Neanderthal hide if he so much as causes that boy a single moment of unhappiness."

She wondered if he knew how heroic he sounded, making himself Joel's champion.

"Road trip it is," she agreed. "I'll be back here with the papers tomorrow morning," she promised.

He missed her already and she hadn't even walked down his driveway yet. It amazed him how much his life had changed in such a very short span of time. How much it had changed and how much that didn't seem to bother him.

He supposed that you never stopped learning.

"Jewel," he called after her. When she turned around in response, he'd already caught up to her. "One for the road," he said in answer to her quizzical look. And then he kissed her.

Jewel was not alone the next morning when she came to pick Chris up. Her mother was sitting in the passenger seat beside her, opting to go in Jewel's car rather than taking the sky-blue-and-white MINI Cooper she loved so dearly.

There could only be one reason for that, Jewel thought. More talk time this way.

She'd called her mother early this morning, asking if she was up to babysitting Joel for the day. Her mother was giving her an enthusiastic "yes" before she even finished the question.

Jewel had hardly backtracked out of her mother's driveway before she started having second thoughts about her impulsive decision. Maybe she should have asked Theresa or Maizie to babysit instead. Cut from the very same fabric as her mother, the two other women at least held themselves in check around her. Not because they weren't each hopelessly enamored with the happily-ever-after scenario they'd all bought into, but because they tried not to come on too strong with someone who wasn't their actual daughter. She knew that neither Theresa or Maizie would be sitting beside her, wearing a smile so smug that it was off the charts.

"Isn't Chris *everything* I said he was?" Cecilia asked, like someone who already had the answer.

"You didn't say anything, Mom," Jewel reminded her tersely. "I should have known better."

"But he's everything I ever wanted for you," Cecilia said with a heartfelt sigh. "Tall, dark and handsome with an intellect that's every bit as impressive as his biceps."

Jewel eased her foot onto the brake at a light that was still yellow in order to look at her mother. "Just when did you see his biceps?" she wanted to know.

In response, Cecilia merely gave her a mysterious smile that would have been the envy of the *Mona Lisa*.

"You don't expect me to give away all my secrets, do you, darling?"

Her mother was making it up as she went along, Jewel concluded, and the more she reacted to what was being said, the more liberties with the truth her mother was going to take.

"No, I certainly don't," she answered with a serious expression. "Just make sure that Joel gets to class and then remember to pick him up. I'm not sure how long we'll be—and *don't,*" she emphasized pointedly, "tell me to stay the night."

Cecilia allowed a touch of despair to enter her voice. "If I have to tell you that, then somewhere along the line I must have gone horribly wrong with your education."

"Your heart's in the right place, Mom," Jewel acknowledged, changing lanes to avoid a slow-moving vehicle, "but your methodology could use a lot of work. Every time you push, I get the overwhelming desire to dig in my heels."

Cecilia frowned. "Even if you miss out on the perfect relationship?"

"Even then." And then she relented slightly. "I didn't say my reaction was a good one, just that I had it." Her mother sighed and Jewel could almost hear the older woman shaking her head. But they'd arrived at Joel's house. Despite the dauntingly long drive that loomed ahead of her, most of it probably in soul-depressing traffic, Jewel cheered herself up with the fact that she wasn't going to have to deal with her mother's penchant for matchmaking for the rest of the day.

Stopping the car, she got out and crossed to the front door. Her mother was right behind her.

Having heard them drive up, Chris opened the door less than half a minute later. "Thanks for doing this, Cecilia."

"My pleasure entirely, Chris," she responded with feeling. "And don't feel you have to come rushing back right away," the woman added. "Joel and I will be just fine holding down the fort until you're here again."

"Where are you going?" Joel wanted to know, drawn to the doorway by the sound of their voices. It was still early and he'd just finished eating breakfast. He didn't need to get ready for school for another twenty minutes.

"Just a little road trip, Joel," Jewel told the boy, opting for the simplest explanation. She'd forgotten how curious he'd become, asking questions until he was satisfied.

"A little road trip to where?"

"Las Vegas," Chris told him.

"Did you know that they have over a thousand chapels in Las Vegas?" Cecilia asked innocently.

Jewel had never bothered doing a head count of the number of chapels in the gambling capital of the country. "I'm sure it's not that many, Mother," Jewel replied tersely, giving her a warning look.

Her mother smiled in response, completely ignoring the "back off" look in her daughter's eyes. "All it takes is one."

Fighting back a wave of embarrassment as she debated whether or not to commit justifiable homicide, Jewel looked at the man she'd come to pick up.

"Let's go before the traffic gets really bad," she said, although she knew it was already too late for that. It was Friday and there were always people trying to get a jump on a long weekend. The traffic would most likely be bumper to bumper.

Unaware of traffic patterns when it came to Vegas, Chris nodded, pausing only to say a few parting words to Joel. "You be good, Joel, and do whatever Mrs. Parnell tells you to do."

"She lets me call her Cecilia," Joel told him happily.

"I'm letting you call her Mrs. Parnell," Chris pointed out, his meaning clear.

"Yes, sir. Mrs. Parnell," Joel repeated.

"Grandma might be a compromise," Cecilia suggested, not quite managing to carry off an innocent expression.

"In what universe?" Jewel challenged, then held up her hand before her mother could utter a comeback. "Never mind. I'm not getting sucked into a debate. We have to go."

Cecilia placed a delicate hand to her chest. "Why Jewel, whatever do you mean?"

Jewel gave her a dark look, but made no reply other than a generic, "See you later," which she actually directed toward Joel before turning on her heel and hurrying out to her vehicle in the driveway.

Chris had just barely made it into the car before she was pulling out of the driveway. She wanted to get away before her mother could say something else to embarrass her beyond all measure.

"You'll have to forgive my mother," she told him, straightening the steering wheel and throwing the car into Drive. "I think she overdosed on her 'Pushy Mom' pills today."

"I hadn't noticed." Chris meant to keep the grin to himself, but he failed, undermining his words to the contrary.

She didn't have to look; she could hear the grin in his voice. "And if I believe that, you have a bridge you'd like to sell me."

He laughed. "No, no bridge. Actually, I'm rather grateful to your mother."

This was going to be good, she thought. "Go ahead, I'm listening."

"Other than the fact that she recommended you as a private investigator, her 'innocent' remarks did manage to get my mind off the reason for this little road trip in the first place." He didn't want to contemplate the fact that, despite Jewel's assurances to the contrary, there was a very real possibility that things could go horribly wrong.

Jewel stole a quick glance in his direction. "Worried?"

"Yes." There was no point in denying it. "Very," he added.

"Don't be." Taking her right hand off the wheel, she patted his knee reassuringly. "Everything's going to turn out just fine."

If only he could believe that. "I forgot, you're an optimist."

"Only way to face life," Jewel answered him with feeling.

"And if Ray decides that he wants to have Joel come live with him?" Despite all his efforts, he couldn't shake himself free of that scenario.

"If it comes to that, optimist or not, I'm also very good at pointing out the downside of things," she assured him. "By the time I get finished with the man, he'll be making an appointment to get a vasectomy within the hour. And you can be sure that he'll be *more* than willing to sign the legal document I have in my purse."

He remembered what she'd said last night. "Then you did get it?"

"We wouldn't be going if I hadn't." Kate hadn't exactly been overjoyed to have Jewel pop up on her doorstep at almost midnight last night, but once she'd been filled in, Kate had understood and forgiven her for her inopportune timing. As had Jackson. "It's all nice and legal and signs over all parental rights to you."

"You do think of everything." There was admiration in his voice.

The corners of her mouth curved. "God knows I try," she told him.

Chris laughed softly and she caught herself reveling in the sound before she silently told herself she had to stop doing that, stop absorbing little bits and pieces of things he did, things he said. Women in love did things like that and that wasn't her. She had her feet firmly planted on the ground, Jewel insisted, and knew what she was doing.

Having fun until the fun ran out.

"I'm going to hold you to that," Chris was saying.

"Fine." *As long as you hold me, I don't care what the reason is.*

The thought galloped through Jewel's mind before she could stop it. It made her nervous.

Because it made her vulnerable.

Chapter Fifteen

Lucky Lady sounded more like a name for an up-and-coming racehorse than a casino, but that was the name the refurbished establishment's new owner had affixed to it. His hope, no doubt, was that luck would indeed materialize, luring a healthy crowd of second-tier gamblers away from the bigger casinos that tended to lavish attention only on very high rollers.

Business, Jewel had learned in her quick investigation, was only fair to moderate. It was the kind of place that someone like Ray Johnson, a.k.a. Dennis Carter, could safely get lost in.

They reached Vegas at a little after one in the afternoon. The high density of traffic migrating from Southern California to the city known for sin and glitter had made the journey particularly draining, especially when it came to a complete standstill.

Entering the city, Jewel turned on her GPS unit. The pathfinding machine glibly told them where to turn and when, allowing Jewel to take in some of the scenery, instead of exclusively searching for street names. What she viewed made her decide that the city's mesmerizing magic only came out after sundown. Vegas in the daytime looked like an aging showgirl. What the night successfully hid, the daylight brought out, accentuating the telltale flaws that time had etched.

"Are you sure you got the right name?" Chris asked, looking at the front of one lesser-known casino after another as they drove past them. "I've never heard of the Lucky Lady."

Neither had she until she'd done a little more research. The high-end casinos were the ones that garnered publicity, but gambling was an across-the-board, equal opportunity addiction and opportunists made the most of it, providing avenues for the rich and the definitely-not-rich alike.

"When was the last time you were in Vegas?" Jewel asked.

Chris paused, trying to remember. "Six, seven years ago," he finally admitted. "Maybe a little longer." He'd gone to attend a convention for university physics professors. He'd come away thinking too much energy was being wasted in one place, but he kept that to himself.

"Things change here daily," she told him. "A year ago, the Lucky Lady was called the Royal Flush or something equally inane. Ray—or Dennis, take your pick—hasn't exactly come up in the world, but at least he's working now." Coming to a red light, she turned to look at him. "Want to stop for lunch first?" she offered.

He shook his head. He doubted if he could have kept it down. But then it occurred to him that he wasn't the only one to consider here. "Unless you do," he amended.

She was hungry, but she could wait. "Business before pleasure," she replied. The light turned green. "According to the map I looked at earlier—"

"Turn right, here," a disembodied voice instructed. "Final destination on right."

"This must be the place," she murmured.

There was one lone valet in a somewhat rumpled uniform sitting on a stool against the wall. When he saw them pull up, he came alive and hurried over to the sedan.

Ordinarily, it was against her basic principles to have someone else do for her what she was perfectly capable of doing for herself. But parking here, even in the daytime, would be tough for a seasoned magician to pull off. Jewel surrendered her vehicle and her keys to the gawky valet who looked as if he'd only begun to shave that morning, accepting a receipt in return.

"Park it near the front," she told the valet. "We won't be long."

The look on the tall, thin young man's face told her that he might be unseasoned, but he'd heard that before. With effort, he slid his long frame into the vehicle and murmured, "Yes, ma'am."

She and Chris walked up to the front doors of the casino in strained silence. She stopped just before entering and looked at him. "Ready?"

No, he wasn't. He would rather have skipped this entirely and just continued with this new life that had been thrust upon him, but he knew that Jewel was right. Not notifying Ray or securing legal custody of his nephew would leave him open to a life fraught with unease. He'd be forever waiting for the other shoe to drop without having so much as a clue when that might be.

"Let's get this over with," he answered.

She nodded, noting that he'd deliberately avoided repeating the word that she had used. Jewel went in first.

They worked their way past the squadron of machines affectionately—and not so affectionately—referred to as one-armed bandits. The minute she spotted the bar, Jewel picked up her pace and crossed to it. Any bartender worth his paycheck knew everyone.

The stocky bartender stopped massaging the slick countertop as she approached and gave her his best smile. "What's your pleasure, little lady?"

"Information," Jewel replied with a smile that matched his. She took out a photograph of Ray she'd printed up from the DMV archives. "Does this man work here?"

The bartender shook his head, clearly about to plead ignorance, when his eyes caught the twenty peeking out from behind the photograph she'd laid down on the bar. Picking up the photograph, he took a closer look.

"Yeah, that's Dennis." Setting the photograph back down, he closed his hand around the twenty.

"Is he here today?" Chris asked.

"Saw him earlier," the other man confirmed, then

pointed off to the right. "He's over there, at the blackjack table. Dealing," he added.

Jewel slipped the photograph back into her pocket. "Thanks."

"Come by anytime," the bartender told her as she walked away. "I'll give you a drink on the house."

"That's probably not all he'll give you," she heard Chris mutter under his breath.

It took an effort for her to suppress the grin that rose to her lips. It almost sounded as if Chris were jealous. But she knew better. Jealousy was for people in a relationship. They were just two ships docked at the same port for a limited time, and she was going to have to keep reminding herself of that until it sank in. Especially since everything appeared to be coming to an end.

As they approached the blackjack table, she noted that Joel's father seemed to be struggling not to appear as bored as he obviously was. Currently, there were two men at his table. One looked as if he'd spent his life perched on a stool at one casino or another, and the other was a couple of decades younger, wet behind the ears and searching for his fifteen minutes with Lady Luck. Both men were watching Ray deal as if their very lives depended on the next turn of the card.

Six-four and stocky—he'd obviously gained weight since he and Rita were an item—with dark hair and small, narrow eyes, Ray looked up as Jewel came to the table. Interest instantly flared in his gaze.

"Take a seat," he told her, his tone low and velvety.

"We came to talk," Chris said, taking his place beside her.

Ray's seductive smile instantly faded. His eyes darted around the two people, as if he expected to see someone else with them. It didn't take much to figure out who it was he was expecting.

Looking around, he called out to someone just to his left. "Kelly, can you take over for me for a few minutes?"

The woman looked annoyed and on the verge of saying no when her eyes came to rest on Chris. An appreciative smile slowly worked its way through the frown.

"Sure, why not?" The smile faded when the man who had caught her attention moved away from the table at the same time that the dealer did.

"How did you find me?" Ray hissed at Chris the moment he'd placed enough space between himself and the other casino employees.

"The credit goes to Jewel," Chris told him, nodding at the woman beside him.

Anger rumbled in Ray's voice and colored his features. "I haven't got any money for Rita or the kid, if that's what you're here about. I'm barely getting by—and I've got a wife to support. I've got a decent enough life now. I ain't going back."

"I'm very happy for you," Chris said flatly, his expression conveying the exact opposite.

"I ain't going back," Ray repeated with more feeling. "You can't make me."

"No one wants you to go back," Jewel assured him, wondering what it was that Chris's sister ever saw in this Neanderthal.

"Then what are you doing here? And where's Rita?"

he asked suspiciously, obviously still thinking she might pop up at any moment.

"Rita died." She could hear the pain in Chris's voice, even though his expression never changed. Rita's ex seemed to be oblivious to it, apparently unaffected by the news.

"Died? Of what?" he asked suspiciously.

"A brain aneurysm," Jewel answered.

"Yeah, well, that's too bad." Ray shrugged carelessly as he glanced back toward his table and the disgruntled woman who was covering for him. "We've all got to go sometime. Look, I've got to get back to the table. I've already taken my break. They don't like you to abuse the rules here."

But Chris wasn't about to let him go just yet. They had unfinished business. "Aren't you even going to ask about Joel?" he demanded.

Ray shrugged again. "What about him?" he asked indifferently. And then his eyes narrowed as a realization occurred to him. "Is that why you're here? To pawn the little wimp off on me?" His mouth twisted as if the very thought of dealing with his son repelled him. "Well, you can just forget about it. My wife's pregnant. She's expecting twins." It was obvious that the news was not a source for celebration for him. "I've got more than I can handle."

"We'll make this quick and painless," Jewel said, getting in his way as he tried to leave again. Fishing around in her purse, she grabbed and held up the papers that Kate had drawn up for her. "Just sign this and you can go on with your life."

Ray frowned as he regarded the document suspiciously. "What's that?"

"Legal papers pertaining to your parental rights to Joel." For the sake of brevity, she summarized the contents. "It says that you're giving them up freely."

Ray's dark eyes darted back and forth from his former brother-in-law to Jewel. "And then I'm not responsible for him anymore?"

"And then you're not responsible for him anymore," Jewel guaranteed, nodding her head.

"Hell, yes, I'll sign it. Give me something to write with," he declared eagerly, feeling his pockets as he searched for a pen.

Taking one out of his breast pocket, Chris thrust it into Ray's hand. "Here."

Ray looked around for a surface to write on, and Jewel turned around, offering up her back for him to use. He lost no time in signing the papers.

"Done," Ray declared, giving her the document and Chris the pen. "Now get the hell away from me before I get in trouble," he snapped.

The look Chris gave him could have shot daggers. "Gladly," he bit off.

Ray turned on his heel, about to walk away. But then he paused and turned around again. "Hey, he's not worth anything is he? The kid?"

"Not in the way you mean," Chris answered coldly. He could envision himself wrapping his hands around the man's thick neck and choking the life out of him. Chris took hold of Jewel's arm, hurrying her away.

"C'mon, I need to get out of here before I do something really stupid."

Jewel found that she had to rush in order to keep up with him. "Like what?" she prodded as they made their way out of the casino.

"Like strangle that piece of dirt with my bare hands."

She'd seen better-matched battles. "He's got about thirty pounds and four inches on you," Jewel pointed out tactfully.

"Rage has got to count for something," Chris retorted.

The last thing she wanted was to have him go ballistic. "Put it behind you, Chris," she urged him. "You've got custody of Joel. That's all that matters."

He took a deep breath and then let it out. The anger he felt on Rita's behalf, as well as Joel's, began to subside a little.

Collecting himself, he corrected her last statement. "Not all."

"A big part of it, then," she amended. This wasn't the time or place to split hairs over semantics. "Why don't we go somewhere, grab a late lunch and celebrate?" she suggested, then added a word that put everything into perspective. "'Dad'?"

For a moment he appeared to be rolling her words over in his head. And then he nodded. "Sounds good to me."

"Great, because I am really starving," she told him, doing her best to sound cheerful and upbeat despite realizing that she'd lost sight of the fact that their association was about to come to an end. If not now, then very, very soon. The goal had been achieved. That meant that she was no longer of any service to him. They could each go their separate ways and move on with their lives, emphasis on *separate*.

"You're awfully quiet," Chris commented. Immediately after having lunch they'd hit the road and, unlike the trip out, were making great time. He'd noticed that as she'd turned on the engine, she'd also turned on the radio. Music, not conversation, had filled the air for the past few hours. "I'm not used to that with you."

She was surprised that it had taken him this long to notice. With a half shrug, she gave him a vague excuse. "Just thinking."

She did her thinking out loud. At least, that was what he'd come to expect. This was something different. "About?"

"My next case."

Next case, as opposed to this one. Was that all this had been to her, he caught himself wondering. Just a case? Now that it was solved, her attention had shifted to another puzzle, another challenge. An uneasy feeling wafted through him.

"You have something lined up?" he asked, trying to discern if he was being paranoid or if he had a good reason to feel this way.

She avoided his eyes and stared at the road straight ahead as she nodded. "Came in a couple of days ago," she added.

"Does that mean you'll be busy?" *And that I won't be able to see you?* he added silently.

"Very." The single word came out in a rush and emphatically.

He felt a chill running down his spine. She was telling him that it was over. Just like that.

"Okay," he said slowly, as if he was tasting the word and found it bitter.

Okay. Chris had accepted the lame excuse she'd given him. Maybe he even welcomed it, she thought. Just like that, without a challenge, without a protest. He was okay with it, okay with not seeing her because she was "busy."

Dammit, what did she expect? She *knew* that their association, that what had happened between them, those few, precious weeks, had all just been temporary. She'd told herself as much over and over again. Hell, she'd walked into this knowing it was finite.

Why couldn't she have gotten the message through to her damn heart?

Jewel let out a long breath slowly, struggling to focus on the road. They'd made excellent time and were almost home. All the traffic had been headed toward Vegas. Hardly anyone was coming back this soon.

And then, before she knew it, the trip was over. Just as their time together was over. She was pulling up in his driveway.

And her mouth felt like cotton.

Chris got out on his side. It took a second before he realized that she wasn't moving. She was still sitting behind the steering wheel. Moreover, the engine was still running.

Rounding the hood, he came over to her side. "Aren't you coming in?"

She wanted to, but it was only putting off the inevitable. Trying to revive something that had already been declared dead. And besides, her mother was inside. One look at her face and her mother would know what was going on. And knowing her, her mother would make some sort of comment. Or worse, try to keep them together.

She wasn't up to that.

"No, I'll pass, thanks." Her voice was flat, devoid of emotion. "I'm kind of tired. Besides, this is your moment," she told him, trying to smile. "Yours and Joel's. I don't want to get in the way."

She was brushing him off, Chris thought. Her mind was obviously made up. He wasn't about to beg and embarrass both of them.

Stepping away from the vehicle, he said, "Don't forget to send me the bill."

Like she cared about the damn money. "Right. When I get around to it," she answered vaguely. "I'm going to be very busy."

"So you said," he acknowledged woodenly.

Jewel pressed her lips together, forbidding herself to cry. "Tell Joel goodbye for me." She threw the car into Reverse. If she stayed a moment longer, threats or no threats, she was going to cry.

Chris turned away, not wanting to watch her leave.

His heart felt like lead in his chest as he unlocked the front door.

There was music playing in the background. Cecilia had the radio on as she was finishing up the dishes. The moment she heard the front door, she hurried toward it and was there as Chris walked in.

"Hi. You're back sooner than I thought," Cecilia said, greeting him with a warm smile. She glanced behind him, but he was already closing the door. "Is Jewel parking the car?"

"No," he answered stoically. "Jewel's on her way home."

"Home?" Cecilia echoed as if the word made no sense to her.

He didn't want to talk. Everything inside him felt shell-shocked. He'd thought…

He'd thought like an idiot, Chris upbraided himself. Jewel was a bright, vibrant woman who thrived on excitement. Who generated it wherever she went. He had to have been crazy to think she would have been satisfied with a college professor for more than a few weeks.

"Yes, she left."

There was a finality to the word, to his tone. Cecilia stared at the young man she had handpicked for her daughter. She knew Jewel inside and out. The parts that weren't like her were like her late husband. If Jewel had left, it was because she was afraid. Afraid of getting hurt. Damn that job of hers.

"And you let her?" Cecilia demanded incredulously. Incensed, she shot straight from the hip. "Have you lost your mind or am I completely wrong about you and you don't care about her? Because, like it or not, my daughter loves you, Chris Culhane. All you have to do is look at her face to know that."

Chris opened his mouth to defend himself and then stopped. Suddenly, all the pieces just came flying together. How could he have been so stupid? So caught up in his own imagined hurt that he hadn't read between the lines? Hadn't seen what was right there in front of him? Cecilia was right. He *had* lost his mind. Temporarily. But it was back now. And he was ready to reclaim what was his.

"Stay with Joel," he tossed over his shoulder, heading for the door.

"No problem." Cecilia hurried after him to lock the door. "Just get it right this time," she called after Chris.

"I fully intend to." It was a pledge to himself. And to Jewel.

Chapter Sixteen

Tears were streaming down her face as she drove. Jewel cursed herself.

She thought she was tougher than this. She would have sworn to it if anyone had asked. But tough people didn't cry when the inevitable happened. Not when they knew it was going to happen all along.

Jewel couldn't stop crying even as she struggled to get herself under control.

She'd been right all along. She *knew* it was going to be like this.

So why did being right hurt so damn much?

It wasn't as if this were a surprise. Sitting on the sidelines, gathering proof, she'd seen it happen time and time again. Two halves of a whole coming apart. Sometimes six months after the marriage, sometimes twenty years. But it happened. Over and over again it happened.

Hadn't she said right from the start that all relationships were doomed?

Okay, not all, she reminded herself, but most. The word *most* had been the culprit, the reason she'd let her guard down. *Most* whispered that there was a chance, however small, that she and Chris could somehow beat the odds.

Who was she kidding?

She wasn't a gambler, not when it came to something like this, to matters of the heart. To forever.

She stifled a sob that tried to break free.

Dammit, she had to stop this, had to stop tearing up and falling apart or else she was going to run into something or cause a collision.

Blowing out a shaky breath, she wiped her eyes with the back of her hand.

Maybe she needed to take a break, a vacation. There *was* no other case; she'd lied to Chris. She only wished there were so that she could get her mind off this soul-wrenching ache she felt in the pit of her belly. She desperately needed something to keep her occupied. But since there was no case, maybe she'd just take off for a few days…

And do what? a small voice in her head demanded. *Think?*

That was all she needed, endless days stretching in front of her with nothing to do but think about how empty she felt inside. How hollow.

Ordinarily, if things were getting her down, or she needed to get away, she would get in touch with Nikki or Kate and go with one of them, or both, for a weekend mini-vacation.

But there was no doing that now. Both of her friends were deeply involved with the men in their lives. Any "getting away" would be done with their fiancés, not her. She was the odd girl out.

How had she become the fifth wheel without even knowing it?

Jewel blinked and looked around. She was on the freeway, heading for home. She didn't even remember getting on the on ramp. Apparently, the car was on automatic pilot, she thought.

As was she.

Maybe it was better that way. She needed to stay numb, removed, until she was finally up to dealing with this.

Until the pain was no longer unbearable.

Chris couldn't quite figure it out. How had Jewel managed to get so far ahead of him in such a short time? Only a couple of minutes had gone by, but by the time he'd come rushing out, she was nowhere in sight.

Jumping into his car, he had to all but floor it to even get a glimpse of her. It took another eight minutes of one eye on the road, the other on the lookout for any police cars, to catch up to her.

When he finally did, pulling abreast of her car, Jewel seemed to be oblivious that he was even there. Whether she really didn't see him or was just pretending, he had no idea. What he *did* know was that he was determined to get her to pull over.

Still driving parallel to her vehicle, Chris rolled down the passenger window, leaned on his horn and shouted, "Pull over!"

Stunned, confused and startled to see him suddenly all but at her side, a whole host of emotions raced through Jewel as she maneuvered her car onto the right shoulder of the freeway. The moment she did, he pulled over, as well, parking behind her.

Getting out of the car, she wondered if there was something wrong with either Joel or her mother, both of whom were still at the house.

"What's wrong?" she asked him the second he got out of his car and headed for her. "Did you forget something?"

The sound of cars whizzing by made it hard to talk above a shout. "Yeah, you."

She raised her voice, certain she'd heard wrong. "What?"

"You," he repeated, reaching her. "I got so caught up in everything that I thought it would just continue going right and then I thought—" This was all getting too complicated. "Never mind what I thought. Your mother set me straight."

She had no idea what he was talking about. "My mother?" This had all started with her mother. When would that woman learn to stop meddling?

"Yes." Even standing next to her, he had to shout to be heard. The noise from the cars all around them swelled. "She asked me if I was crazy."

He was still not making any sense, she thought. "And this set you straight?"

"Yes."

She shook her head, but that didn't clear it. Or change things. She just wanted to get away. "What are you talking about?"

Traffic was slowing down now, as motorists began to watch the minidrama playing out on the shoulder of the road.

"Your mother made me realize that I was crazy to let you go without a fight."

"'Let me go'?" she echoed in disbelief. "I thought it was pretty clear that you were trying to tell me it was over."

"Where did you get that idea?" he demanded incredulously. "You were the one who called this just another case."

She *was* guilty of that, she thought. "This *wasn't* just another case, but I didn't want you to think that I expected something."

"What if I expected something?"

She shook her head, unable to make the words out. "What?"

"What if *I* expected something?" he repeated, raising his voice even more.

Her heart refused to settle down and beat normally. "Like what?" she heard herself asking.

"Like spending the rest of my life with you." He took her hands into his. "I'm old-fashioned, Jewel. I don't want to just sleep with you. I want to wake up with you, have breakfast with you, make plans with you—I love you and I want to marry you. You've filled my life the way I never knew was possible. Don't make me feel empty again."

Anything too good to be true wasn't—hadn't that been the first thing she'd ever learned? So why was she rooting for Chris's side, praying he'd say something to convince her?

"Now," she told him. "You want to marry me now, but once whatever you're feeling right at this moment vanishes, once you think things over—"

"I'll still want to marry you," he insisted. "And I'll still want to *be* married to you."

And then, amid the snaking evening traffic, on the shoulder of the road, Chris took one of her hands in his and got down on one knee. "Jewel Parnell, will you marry me?"

Self-conscious, aware that traffic was at a virtual standstill and every set of eyes were now on both of them, she tugged on his hand. "Chris, please, get up," she pleaded.

But he shook his head, remaining where he was. "Not until you tell me you love me and say yes."

She looked up, as if searching the sky for strength. "Of course I love you. I wouldn't be this miserable if I didn't love you."

"*Love* and *miserable*—not exactly the two words I wanted to hear in the same sentence," he told her. "Again, will you marry me?"

She pressed her lips together. Could he actually be serious? About wanting her for all time? "I don't have a choice in the matter?" she asked.

His answer was short and firm. "Nope."

She was losing the battle, but she gave it one more try. "You don't know what you're saying."

"That's where you're wrong. I'm a physicist. I *always* know what I'm saying."

He had no idea how much she wanted to believe him. How much she wanted to be convinced. But she didn't want to wake up some morning only to find him gone. "You haven't thought this through."

"Oh, yes, I have," he contradicted. "Would you like to see the flowchart?"

He got her then. "You made a flowchart?"

He grinned. "With colors and everything."

A motorist leaned out of his car and shouted, "Hey, lady, say yes already!" To underscore his point, he hit his horn, hard. The sound was echoed over and over again as other drivers joined in.

Within moments, there was a cacophony of car horns beeping.

Dammit, she was melting. *Please don't let me regret this.* "You really want to marry me?"

He nodded, his eyes solemn. "I really want to marry you."

"And *stay* married to me?" she emphasized.

"And stay married to you," he echoed.

She let out a long breath slowly. She was going to follow her heart. He was right, she had no choice. "Then I guess I'd better say yes."

He rose to his feet, still holding her hand. "Sounds good to me," he told her before kissing her.

The sound of blaring horns grew louder, but this time, it was the drivers' way of cheering.

At least, that was the way the evening news reported the story later that night when Cecilia taped it. She fully intended to share the tape with her future grandchildren someday.

Epilogue

Joel's eyes moved from his uncle to the woman he'd come to adore. The woman he'd secretly been afraid was going to leave. Except now they were saying something different to him. Something that made him feel very excited.

"You're going to marry my uncle?" he finally asked Jewel in a small voice. That was what they'd been saying to him. That and all this stuff about permission. That's why he was confused. Grown-ups never asked a kid for permission to do anything.

Jewel wanted to marry Chris with all her heart, but there was more than herself to consider here. She knew that. Knew, too, how important it was to feel as if you mattered. Even if you were only five. Feelings had no age limits.

She wanted Joel to know that he mattered. To both of them. And he always would.

"Only if you say yes," she told him.

Joel looked at her, still a tiny bit confused. "You want me to marry you, too?"

Exchanging glances with Chris, Jewel stifled a laugh as she looked back to the boy. "In a way, yes. If I marry your uncle, we're going to be a family, Joel. You, your uncle and me."

"Is that okay with you, Joel?" Chris asked. He looked as serious as Joel ever remembered him looking—except that there was a smile in his eyes. A smile that made Joel feel warm all over.

A family. He, his uncle and Jewel. A real family. He liked the way that sounded. Liked the way that felt in his stomach.

"Okay," he told Jewel. "I'll marry you, too." And then he put one stipulation on his consent. "But Uncle Chris does all the kissing."

Chris laughed as he pulled them both into his arms. "You got it, Joel."

And then, to show his nephew he meant it, he kissed his bride-to-be.

* * * * *

Don't miss Marie Ferrarella's 200th book,
CAVANAUGH REUNION,
Available August 31, 2010
from Silhouette Romantic Suspense.

Silhouette®

COMING NEXT MONTH

Available August 31, 2010

SPECIAL EDITION

REQUEST YOUR FREE BOOKS!

2 FREE NOVELS PLUS 2 FREE GIFTS!

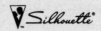

SPECIAL EDITION

Life, Love and Family!

YES! Please send me 2 FREE Silhouette® Special Edition® novels and my 2 FREE gifts (gifts are worth about $10). After receiving them, if I don't wish to receive any more books, I can return the shipping statement marked "cancel." If I don't cancel, I will receive 6 brand-new novels every month and be billed just $4.24 per book in the U.S. or $4.99 per book in Canada. That's a saving of 15% off the cover price! It's quite a bargain! Shipping and handling is just 50¢ per book.* I understand that accepting the 2 free books and gifts places me under no obligation to buy anything. I can always return a shipment and cancel at any time. Even if I never buy another book from Silhouette, the two free books and gifts are mine to keep forever.

235/335 SDN E5RG

Name	(PLEASE PRINT)
Address	Apt. #
City	State/Prov.	Zip/Postal Code

Signature (if under 18, a parent or guardian must sign)

Mail to the **Silhouette Reader Service**:
IN U.S.A.: P.O. Box 1867, Buffalo, NY 14240-1867
IN CANADA: P.O. Box 609, Fort Erie, Ontario L2A 5X3

Not valid for current subscribers to Silhouette Special Edition books.

Want to try two free books from another line?
Call 1-800-873-8635 or visit www.morefreebooks.com.

* Terms and prices subject to change without notice. Prices do not include applicable taxes. N.Y. residents add applicable sales tax. Canadian residents will be charged applicable provincial taxes and GST. Offer not valid in Quebec. This offer is limited to one order per household. All orders subject to approval. Credit or debit balances in a customer's account(s) may be offset by any other outstanding balance owed by or to the customer. Please allow 4 to 6 weeks for delivery. Offer available while quantities last.

Your Privacy: Silhouette is committed to protecting your privacy. Our Privacy Policy is available online at www.eHarlequin.com or upon request from the Reader Service. From time to time we make our lists of customers available to reputable third parties who may have a product or service of interest to you. If you would prefer we not share your name and address, please check here. ☐

Help us get it right—We strive for accurate, respectful and relevant communications. To clarify or modify your communication preferences, visit us at www.ReaderService.com/consumerschoice.

SSE10R

*Enjoy a sneak peek at fan favorite Molly O'Keefe's
Harlequin Superromance miniseries,*
THE NOTORIOUS O'NEILLS, *with*
TYLER O'NEILL'S REDEMPTION,
*available September 2010
only from Harlequin Superromance.*

Police chief Juliette Tremblant recognized the shape of the
man strolling down the street—in as calm and leisurely
fashion as if it were the middle of the day rather than
midnight. She slowed her car, convinced her eyes were
playing tricks on her. It had been a long time since Tyler
O'Neill had been seen in this town.

As she pulled to a stop at the curb, he turned toward her,
and her heart about stopped.

"What the hell are you doing here, Tyler?"

"Well, if it isn't Juliette Tremblant." He made his way
over to her, then leaned down so he could look her in the
eye. He was close enough to touch.

Juliette was not, repeat, *not* going to touch Tyler O'Neill.
Not with her fingers. Not with a ten-foot pole. There would
be no touching. Which was too bad, since it was the only
way she was ever going to convince herself the man standing
in front of her—as rumpled and heart-stoppingly handsome
now as he'd been at sixteen—was real.

And not a figment of all her furious revenge dreams.

"What are you doing back in Bonne Terre?" she asked.

"The manor is sitting empty," Tyler said and shrugged,
as though his arriving out of the blue after ten years was
casual. "Seems like someone should be watching over the
family home."

"You?" She laughed at the very notion of him being here
for any unselfish reason. "Please."

He stared at her for a second, then smiled. Her heart fluttered against her chest—a small mechanical bird powered by that smile.

"You're right." But that cryptic comment was all he offered.

Juliette bit her lip against the other questions.

Why did you go?

Why didn't you write? Call?

What did I do?

But what would be the point? Ten years of silence were all the answer she really needed.

She had sworn off feeling anything for this man long ago. Yet one look at him and all the old hurt and rage resurfaced as though they'd been waiting for the chance. That made her mad.

She put the car in gear, determined not to waste another minute thinking about Tyler O'Neill. "Have a good night, Tyler," she said, liking all the cool "go screw yourself" she managed to fit into those words.

It seems Juliette has an old score to settle with Tyler.
Pick up TYLER O'NEILL'S REDEMPTION
to see how he makes it up to her.
Available September 2010,
only from Harlequin Superromance.

Silhouette® *Desire*

New York Times and USA TODAY
bestselling author

BRENDA JACKSON

brings you

WHAT A WESTMORELAND WANTS,

another seductive Westmoreland tale.

Part of the Man of the Month series

Callum is hopeful that once he gets
Gemma Westmoreland on his native turf
he will wine and dine her with a seduction plan
he has been working on for years—one that
guarantees to make her his.

Available September wherever books are sold.

**Look for a new Man of the Month
by other top selling authors each month.**

Always Powerful, Passionate and Provocative.